THE AUTOMATON EMPRESS

A STEAMPUNK ADVENTURE MYSTERY

LADY GEORGIA BRUNEL MYSTERIES
BOOK TWO

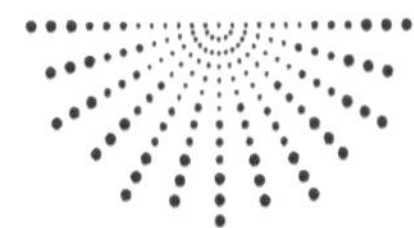

SHELLEY ADINA

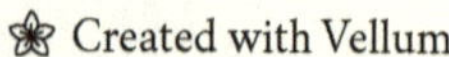 Created with Vellum

"*The Clockwork City* delivers a steampunk mystery with a tick of romance. It rings with charm and a thrilling amount of action! The two ladies Brunel prove to be a resourceful duo and with the help of some well written and well connected secondary characters, their sleuthing skills are put to the test."

— *IND'TALE MAGAZINE*, CROWNED HEART OF EXCELLENCE REVIEW

"I always love a well-written steampunk mystery that is clean, and *The Clockwork City* definitely fits all these criteria. The story is engaging, and the cast of characters play well together even if they aren't playing nice."

— BLOOMING WITH BOOKS

"Shelley Adina is quickly becoming a go-to author for fun, clean steampunk adventures! This delightful mystery completely pulled me in and had me quickly turning the pages. It's a fantastic introduction to a new series I'm looking forward to reading more of."

— MELISSA'S BOOKSHELF

THE AUTOMATON EMPRESS

CHAPTER ONE

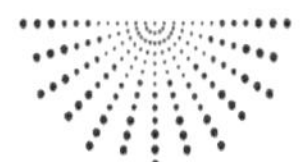

KASTANIENHOF, MUNICH

Monday, May 13, 1895
1:00 p.m.

I must say, I have never been summoned to an audience with an empress before. Not even Queen Victoria." Georgia Brunel, Lady Langford, sat on the edge of the sofa, doing her best not to wrinkle her white waist of Brussels lace and the sapphire gabardine skirt and fashionably trimmed jacket that Lady Louise Thorne's maid had so carefully pressed.

"I still think it is most improper to appear before the Empress of Prussia in a walking costume." Millicent Brunel sniffed—her only movement, for she too feared wrinkling her own burgundy suit with its white cuffs and collar.

Louise breezed into the sitting room, pinning on her hat, in time to hear. "Since you may find Her Imperial Majesty dressed in anything from a pair of bloomers to a canvas pinafore to a partly fitted ballgown—accessorized by a seamstress still busily pinning—I think you both look very presentable. Come along. I shall pilot the landau to Nymphenburg myself."

"Poor Cora," Millie said as they bowled down the broad avenue lined with the chestnut trees that gave the Thorne estate its name—Kastanienhof. "I am sorry she had to return to the Lycée. She so wanted to come."

"My daughter has missed far too much school recently to do so," Louise said crisply, "thanks to my late husband's spiriting her off to Venice to put her life in peril."

Georgia could understand the deep-seated, unresolved rage that had produced this remark, and forgave the poor taste in making it. Lady Thorne had been a heroine throughout the whole affair in Venice—one could only imagine the wounds in her heart from her husband's betrayal. They would need time and peace in which to heal.

And a circle of friends who could empathize and stand with her.

She turned the conversation only slightly. "Cora will miss her friend Marcus. I believe *Foresight* was to have lifted yesterday. What an odd thing for Mr van Meere to have sent a note to you, Millie. Are you certain that you will not satisfy our curiosity about its contents?"

Millie's mouth firmed, as though the answer would continue to be no, and then relaxed. "Very well," she said reluctantly. "But if you disagree with my reply, you are to keep it to yourselves."

"You have my word," Louise said over the singing putter of the landau. "But do speak up. I don't want to miss a thing. This is all so intriguing—I have never known Cornelius to write so much as a parts list to any woman."

Millie extracted a sheet of paper from her pocketbook,

folded in a complicated design that could only have been done as a favor by Marcus Seacombe, who was eleven and an enthusiast of puzzles, sprockets, and other moving parts.

"Dear Miss Brunel,

I hope you will excuse this method of communication, but I found I could not leave Bavaria without at least making the attempt. Seacombe advises me that one must ask permission before this sort of operation commences. Rather like asking the coyote if one might stalk it before one begins, but ... begging your pardon—I did not mean to compare you to a varmint, even metaphorically."

"Good heavens," Georgia said, sagging back against the upholstered cushion. "If this is how the man begins a letter to a lady, how on earth will he conclude?"

"On the contrary, I find you to be a woman of intelligence, beauty, and sheer ~~dam~~ dashed pluck. I should like to correspond with you. I have not corresponded with nor enjoyed physical congress with—"

The landau hitched as Louise Thorne lost her grip on the acceleration bar. She recovered it with hasty skill and regained control of the steering pedals. "I beg your pardon. Please continue."

"—any female since the death of my wife twenty years ago. So as you might imagine, it has taken a sleepless night and earnest conversation with Seacombe—"

"I do not see that *he* is such an authority on the pursuit of a woman," grumbled Georgia, her pride and her feelings still stinging from said gentleman's departure. *Gentleman* being an exceedingly loose term. He had abstracted his son from Kastanienhof yesterday without so much as a good morning. Or a good-bye.

"Will you restrain yourselves?" Millie demanded in exasperation. "May I read, or not?"

"Do go ahead, dearest," Georgia said meekly.

"—to screw up my courage enough to ask. If you would like to embark upon the uncharted skies of a correspondence, please send a word by the courier, who has been instructed to wait for a reply. Upon receipt, my crew have orders to lift. No matter the nature of the reply, I offer you and Lady Langford a standing invitation to Rancho del Jinete Fantasma in the Texican Territory at your convenience, though I have a feeling the young lady may find the climate at Seacombe's place on the Pecos more salubrious."

Georgia pressed her lips together to prevent a smile at being referred to as *the young lady*. She supposed that to a man of his and Millie's ages, despite her being thirty-eight and the mother of an Oxford scholar, she was still practically an ingenue. As for the climate at Dustin Seacombe's ranch or any other location he occupied, such speculation was entirely beneath her notice.

"I remain, in all sincerity, yours very truly,
    Cornelius van Meere, RSE"

"My, my," said Louise as the white, classically elegant buildings of Nymphenburg Palace swam into view behind their black iron gates. "Do I dare ask the nature of your reply to this astonishing missive?"

"You will plague me until I tell you, so I may as well do so first as last," Millie said, folding up the letter and replacing it in her pocketbook. "I gave him my permission."

Georgia's astonishment was so great that she was hardly aware of the gates being opened for them, nor of the beautiful gardens and fountains of a vast park sliding past the viewing ports of the landau. "You did?"

For the first time, Millie's dignity faltered. "I know I said you were to keep your opinion to yourself, but … do you think I did right?"

"Why—I hardly know," Georgia stammered. "The two of you are not much acquainted."

"How would you know? You were in gaol, and when you weren't, you were cavorting in lagoons with krakens and stealing airships."

Valid points, all.

Perhaps the best way to answer Millie's question was to ask another. "But are you prepared for such a correspondence to—to proceed? To bear fruit?"

"What do you mean?"

"She means, are you prepared for the correspondence to become a courtship," Louise said over her shoulder. "The man must be smitten. I have known him long enough to guess that. And if you have given your permission for the one, then he may believe you are amenable to the other. To being courted, in short, by a multimillionaire with a reputation as a hermit living alone on a ranch of a hundred thousand acres, but who despite that has friends at the highest levels of government in several countries, and is one of the foremost engineers in the world."

"Oh," Millie said, her usually straight spine wilting like a flower in the sun. She did not say another word as they drew up to a broad set of pristine white steps. She looked rather like someone who has dived into a pool and changed their mind halfway down.

Nymphenburg Palace was laid out with a grand central edifice, and two smaller edifices with courts and pillars and colonnades to either side. It was known as the Versailles of the Tyrol for the gardens, trees, and walks that extended for miles to both front and rear. In the lake that reflected the front of the grand palace, swans floated like elegant clouds. It was illegal even to approach the royal swans, and Georgia imagined many a small boy hustled out of harm's way after so much as glancing at one resting on the lawn.

Lady Thorne was recognized instantly by the waiting attaché, and they were escorted to the imperial audience chamber. Unlike the actual Versailles, which Georgia had only seen in pictures and paintings, the palace was not an explosion of Baroque excess, but designed instead in the more restrained Empire style. Oh, there was plenty of gold leaf, but it was meant, she imagined, to act as a frame for royal personages, not to intimidate the visitor to the point of speechlessness.

Napoleon, she had learned in her history lessons, had been obsessed with technology, and in his determination to conquer neighboring kingdoms such as Bavaria, had spent his money on airships and behemoths of war, not on something as irrelevant as interior decoration. He had, she remembered with an inner flash of amusement, been brought down by two young women. How fitting.

After that, the Hapsburg dynasty who had been in collusion with Napoleon had crumbled. The Prussian Empire had risen to dignity and power, this palace being one of the showpieces of that period.

On her previous visit, which had immediately followed her panicked arrival in Munich, Georgia had been shown at once to the empress's office overlooking an orangerie. Today, their audience was to be more formal. The audience chamber was large enough for hundreds, but this morning contained only fifty or so to hear them announced. Their escort pointed out certain luminaries—the Minister of Transportation and Export, the Consul General of Hungary, and Count Ferdinand von Zeppelin, who had visited England several times. Georgia had been introduced at some reception or other, so she curtsied and he bowed.

"Lady Langford, a pleasure," he murmured. "I see you are a friend of our esteemed Lady Thorne." He took Louise's hand. "Our condolences, my dear friend, upon the death of your husband."

"Thank you, Graf," Louise said, using the German equivalent of his title.

His keen gaze moved to Millie. "Miss Brunel, may I ask—are you a relation of the esteemed engineer?"

"A cousin, sir," she replied. They were the first words she had spoken since the revelations in the landau.

"Such an illustrious family," he beamed. "But I will not keep you. The empress, you see, is waiting."

Georgia took a deep breath and straightened her spine. Formality was always disconcerting. At the base of the steps to the dais, all three curtseyed to the floor. With a languid motion of the hand, the empress bade them rise.

She was a young woman, not even thirty, with a wandlike waist and perfect posture. Her skin was like porcelain, her eyes the blue of delphiniums in summer. Her hair was piled upon her head and an arched gold coronet encrusted with tiny round jewels—diamonds, rubies, emeralds—rested upon it. Her gown … Georgia took it in from sleeves to train and nearly swooned.

"You are very welcome to our court today, Lady Langford, Miss Brunel," she said pleasantly. "It has been some time since I have seen you, Lady Thorne."

"I—yes, it has," Louise managed. "You had requested that we wait upon you together, to report the events of the last several days in Venice."

"Yes, so I recall."

Louise glanced over her shoulder. "Such a report is rather sensitive, Ma'am, given the involvement of my husband in his capacity as diplomat."

"Quite so. We will adjourn to my private sitting room. Perhaps you would care for some refreshment."

It was not a question. Wordlessly, they followed the empress around the throne and through a door concealed behind the draperies at the rear. The room into which they were decanted could have been any gentlewoman's sitting room, with comfortable sofas, paintings on the walls, and pale blue silk draperies that fell twelve feet from ceiling to floor on either side of four sets of windows.

"Would you ring the bell?"

Millie looked over her shoulder, and in the absence of so

much as a footman, pulled the length of tapestry next to the tiled fireplace, which was laid but not lit.

The empress seated herself, her cream silk skirts puffing up around her. "Please begin."

It was difficult to know *where* to begin, given that the empress was already in possession of several of the facts, so Georgia left it up to Louise, who rapidly and with economy outlined the events in which she had been involved, then invited Georgia and Millie to fill in their side, as well as what they had discovered about Sir Francis Thorne's activities. Both she and Millie kept quiet about the krakens, however. It did not seem quite … proper … to speak of such things outside of the scientific community, even though the empress was known far and wide to be an engineer of great brilliance. Some even thought it had been a mistake to allow her to inherit the throne when her talents clearly lay not in diplomacy and governance, but in the laboratory. However, as the saying went, blood will out. One could not avoid the laws of inheritance when it came to crowns.

"So you see, Ma'am," Louise concluded, "I quite agree with you that some action must be taken with regard to those in high places in Venice. They cannot simply suborn a diplomat of the British Empire, use him for their own ends, and dispose of him when that use is ended."

"No indeed," the empress said serenely.

Georgia could not reconcile the young woman she had met the other day—who had received her in a stained pinafore, clearly having been dragged away from her laboratory, with this beautifully turned-out woman whose self-possession was almost eerie.

"It is not my place to say, of course, what your course of

action ought to be," Louise went on. "I can only express my hope that you might correspond with Queen Victoria and take her advice upon the matter. She and Prince Albert, after all, have several decades' experience in the management of the Doges of Venice. I understand the latter tend to be unruly, and prone to acting as though they are the only nation worth mentioning on the planet."

"Yes, I have the same understanding. Very well. I shall communicate with Her Majesty and we will agree upon what is to be done." The empress rose. "Thank you for coming to see me."

"We are grateful for your time." Georgia and Millie sank into curtseys.

"I do hope we will see you at the Maifest Ball on Saturday the eighteenth. I am very much looking forward to it."

Louise's face went slack, though she managed to conceal it as she rose from her curtsey. "I—I am in mourning, Ma'am, but if you will send an invitation to Kastanienhof, I am sure that Lady Langford and Miss Brunel would be only too happy to attend. I know your Bavarian subjects look forward to the May Festival each year."

"Consider it done. Now I must return to my duties. My attaché will escort you out."

Within minutes, they were once again upon the clean white steps being handed in to the landau by their expressionless guide. When the wings were safely closed, Louise let out a gasp as she ignited the boiler. "We must do something. This is dreadful. I do not know what the palace is playing at, but this cannot be allowed to go on."

"What cannot be allowed?" Millie asked. "Did you find the empress to be out of spirits?"

With a yelp of laughter that sounded almost hysterical, Louise pushed out the acceleration bar and the landau puttered around the huge carriage circle and off down the broad avenue lined with roses preparing to bloom.

"I did not find the empress at all," she said at last, passing fountains and gardens at a pace much more rapid than when they had entered.

"What on earth do you mean?" Georgia demanded.

"That was not Empress Christina von Waldemar und Mecklenburg. That was her automaton. I have worked on it myself—I would know it anywhere. What I would very much like to know is, why is it masquerading as its creator, and why is everyone going along with it?" She took a deep breath, clearly striving for calm. "What has happened to Christina?"

CHAPTER TWO

By the time they reached Kastanienhof, Lady Thorne had recovered herself somewhat, if only because Georgia and Millie were in the landau and it would be inhospitable of her to pilot them into a tree or down a hillside. But as they sat down to tea—which had never arrived during their private audience—she was still pale and anxious.

Georgia took the liberty of pouring, lest the teapot be in some danger.

"Might there not be a reasonable explanation?" Millie asked, accepting a cup and choosing a hazelnut petit-four from the selection on the tiered plate. "Perhaps this was to be a dress rehearsal for some grander event. The audience chamber was nearly empty, and you are known to be a friend to the empress."

"What event would necessitate an automaton impersonating a royal person?" Louise ate a raspberry tart, but Georgia was nearly certain it could have been a dung beetle for all the notice she took of it.

"I do not know," Millie said, "but there must be no end of

dull engagements where a duplicate of oneself would be useful. Waving from balconies, having debutantes presented, that sort of thing. She may simply want to do something more interesting and chose this as a solution."

"She was certainly very much as you had described her when I saw her on Saturday. And I agree the impersonation did not seem to bother anyone," Georgia added. "Either they did not know it was the automaton, or she has substituted the thing before and they are used to it."

"I find that difficult to believe," Louise said after a gulp of tea. "She called it her plaything, and the last I knew, it was in her laboratory at Linderhof. I must say, she has refined its behavior considerably since I saw it a month ago. She must have been working day and night."

"But to what end?" Millie asked. "Empires do not administer themselves. Useful or not, her duty must come before any plaything, to say nothing of courtesy. You are, after all, her friend. She would appear in person for you, if no one else."

"So one would think," Georgia said. "But even in our own royal house, duty often did not apply. We had the Tinkering Prince's Regency, for instance."

With a nod, Millie acknowledged the truth of this. "Lady Thorne, I can see by your distress that you do not believe the empress substituted the automaton to give herself more time for her own pursuits."

Louise shook her head. "I believe darker forces are at work."

Georgia sat up, alarmed. "What forces? You don't suppose the Doge has agents here, do you?"

"I know for a fact that he does."

Georgia gasped. Just when they thought they had escaped!

"You saw her on Saturday, Georgia. Did you notice anything unusual? Did she seem afraid? Burdened? Distracted?"

"Since I had never met her before, I do not know what might constitute *unusual,*" Georgia admitted. "Our meeting was brief—only a few minutes in which to apprise her of what had happened to you, and to ask for her help if it were needed. She was infuriated by the transportation minister's gall in imprisoning me in his attempt to coerce you. But she did not seem afraid. Indeed, her concern turned straightaway to the repairs to *Thetis.*"

"That is like her." Louise's fine brows pleated in a frown. "From the beginning of her reign, Christina has had a gift for … ruffling feathers. She is wildly intelligent—far more than I. As an engineer, she can give Cornelius van Meere a run for his money. If there were anyone less interested in wearing the crown than she, I don't know who it would be." She stopped. "Even that idiot Rupert von Mecklenburg."

"Who is he when he is at home?" Millie inquired.

"The heir presumptive to the throne."

"Oh dear." Georgia had read of him in the papers. "He's a cousin or something, isn't he? Lives to ride and hunt and drink copious quantities of spirits?"

"The very one," Louise said. "I have met him on a few occasions. He lives in what the royal family call a *lodge,* but is really a small palace in the forest. Convenient for shooting anything that moves and bringing in cancan dancers for entertainment. If Christina dies unmarried and childless, he will inherit."

Georgia pictured someone like the present Prince of

Wales, who was a notorious womanizer and enjoyed his share of spirits, too.

"The two of them are supposed to host the Maifest Ball," Louise went on, "which I must say would be enough to make me create an automaton, if only so it could relieve me of the honor of dancing with him. The feet on that man!"

Mention of the ball had returned Georgia's thoughts to the automaton. "It is so lifelike," she murmured. "The skin, the eyes, the voice … Empress Christina is not merely an engineer. She must be a genius."

"She is that," Louise agreed. "The skin was the most difficult. Not only had she to find a compound that would stretch to create facial expressions, but it had to be tough enough to withstand the machinery beneath." She seemed to catch herself. "I am certain that she is not a willing party to the substitution—she may not even know about it. Someone may have removed her for their own purposes, and substituted the automaton because it was conveniently to hand."

"Removed her … to what end?" Millie asked.

Georgia tried to imagine anyone removing Queen Victoria against her will, and her imagination failed her. "Is there some point of policy that said party disagrees with?" she wondered aloud. "Some political matter that would be solved by the head of state's absence?"

"I do not think so. Parliament's term is nearly over," Louise said. "That is the purpose of the Maifest Ball—to celebrate its successful conclusion. Afterward, everyone departs for their country estates or takes to the air to travel."

"That doesn't sound very awful," Millie said. "What about this Rupert fellow? It stands to reason he would want her out of the way."

"If he does, he might have to stir himself to actually think, to say nothing of acting on behalf of the empire once he had achieved his ends," Louise said acidly. "He is an archduke, very popular, according to the papers, but I have never seen evidence of his coveting the crown. Unless it were buried in a beefsteak."

"Still, he is one possibility," Millie persisted.

"But we are only guessing," Georgia said. "What would Sherlock Holmes do?"

Louise's brows rose. "Do you make a habit of consulting fictional characters?"

"He is a very useful fictional character," Millie said stoutly. "He helps one employ logic and observation, if emotion does not serve."

"Logic would dictate that we are making a wedding cake out of a petit four," Georgia pointed out as she selected one from the cake stand. "The empress could have been indisposed, and substituted the automaton for a lark."

"I do not like being asked to disclose my husband's treachery as part of a lark." Louise sat back and crossed her arms. "The automaton can remember. Not as we do, but it can repeat what has been said verbatim, if commanded."

"That might be useful to … dark forces," Georgia said slowly. "Can't you see the Doge ordering someone to make it repeat what it has heard in the empress's Cabinet meetings and such? One would only need to write down such a report and pop it in a tube."

Louise had gone pale. "Please, that might be only too possible. Let us not speculate or I shall be ill."

"We must not have that," Millie said briskly. "The truth is that we three are English citizens and none of this really has anything to do with us. If the Prussians have misplaced their empress, it is their job to locate her, is it not?"

"Don't you find it odd they don't seem to have noticed she has *been* misplaced?" Georgia asked. "I am not disputing the truth of what you say, dearest. But if she had played such a joke on someone as august as Count von Zeppelin, or her own ministers, wouldn't they have mentioned it to us? Let us in on the joke before we had our private audience?"

"On the contrary, they behaved as if she were there in person," Louise mused. "The automaton is a marvel. From the steps of the dais, I thought it was Christina—though heaven knows that Worth gown is wildly out of character. It should have been my first clue."

The Worth gown. Georgia sighed with longing.

"It was not until we sat down with her that I knew," Louise said. "But by then it was too late. I had to give the report she requested. Otherwise, had anyone made the automaton repeat the contents of our meeting, they would have found it odd that it consisted solely of remarks about the weather."

"*I* thought it odd that tea never arrived," Millie said, selecting a tart laden with fruit. "But then, I suppose that would have given away the game. Automatons, one presumes, do not eat."

"But they must be dressed," Georgia said suddenly, sitting straighter. "Is everyone at court laboring under a mass delusion? Where were her ladies? Surely one of them must have asked herself why she was dressing the empress's plaything in a Worth gown."

"At least it wouldn't be ruined," Louise pointed out, with an air of looking on the bright side. "She has spoiled many a lovely dress with gear oil, or torn it on machinery, or burned it on a Bunsen flame. That is why she works in a pinafore now. Canvas is more difficult to damage."

"Do you know any of her ladies?" Georgia persisted. "We might ask."

"Georgia," Millie began in a warning tone, "I repeat, this is none of our business. Our business is to return to England in time to welcome Teddy when he comes down from Oxford."

Georgia subsided, helpless in the face of the truth. Half of her yearned to see her boy again, to hear all about his tutors and his lessons, and to tell him in turn about Venice. He would love the story of the krakens. The other half of her could feel Louise's palpable distress at the inexplicable absence of a woman she considered a friend.

"Perhaps the very least we could do is make one or two discreet inquiries, to satisfy ourselves," she said at last. "It shouldn't take long, and then we can see about booking train tickets to Calais."

"Discreet inquiries with whom?" Millie said.

"I know the Landgräfin Winter," Louise said thoughtfully. "She is Christina's Lady of the Wardrobe, highest ranking of all her ladies, and her closest aide. If anyone would know why the automaton was trundled out in Christina's place, it would be she. All the ladies in waiting have rooms at the palace. Shall I send a note?"

"If there is a perfectly logical explanation, you will bear the brunt of the embarrassment," Millie warned her.

"I think I have a good excuse." She smoothed her black silk skirts. "Mourning, you see, covers a multitude of sins. Even a supposedly addled mind."

"I beg your pardon, Lady Thorne," Millie said meekly. "I did not mean—"

"No, you were quite right. And I asked you before to call me Louise."

Millie smiled. "Old habits are difficult to break."

"New friendships are an excellent reason to break old habits." Louise smiled back, but her eyes had begun to snap. "I confess I am still wrestling with my feelings about being married to a man who could be coerced by a foreign government into stealing my child from me. Until I resolve those feelings, I shall be happy to blame any number of peccadilloes on mourning."

That much agreed upon, she wrote a note requesting a few minutes of the lady's time, and dispatched it by tube to the palace. Georgia had no idea how long a reply might take, so she told her hostess and Millie she would walk about the grounds and get some fresh air.

The grounds, she had to admit, were beautiful enough to soothe any woman's soul. It was not only the chestnut avenue whose trees were festooned with cones of creamy blossom. There were more species of rhododendron than she knew existed, a riot of purple, pink, and white, all appearing to grow wild. Around the manor house, lilacs breathed scent into the May air. The terrace at the rear of the house overlooked a lake whose convenient walking path decided her, and she set off.

She couldn't remember when she had last been alone to think. Millie would be the first to encourage her to enjoy time alone, though she herself abhorred it. As the maiden aunt shuffled from one relative's home to another, Millie had had her fill of solitude before she had come to Langford Park and found its mistress bruised, hopeless, and despairing. Somehow two injured women had given each other strength, and they had prevailed in the end.

A fish jumped in the lake and startled Georgia out of the past.

Fish reminded her of Venice. How on earth had they survived Venice? One thing was certain—both she and Millie had changed as a result. Perhaps that was why she was ready to entertain this matter of the empress, and Millie was just as happy to stay out of it. In either case, though, friendship seemed to lie at its core. Without friendship, Louise might just shrug her shoulders and return to her own laboratory. Without friendship, she and Millie might leave her to it.

But friendship existed now, and could change lives in small ways and great.

After all, how difficult could it be to locate the best-known person in the kingdom, whose face was on the currency, for goodness sake? Someone must know something, and it was almost certain that a lady in waiting would. At least it was a place to begin.

A cloud passed over the sun, and with a quick intake of breath, she tilted her head back, shading her eyes.

Oh, you are such a fool.

For of course it was not *Foresight*'s massive fuselage, blotting out the sun as it made a farewell pass over Kastanienhof.

Disgusted with herself, she picked up her pace. She was halfway around the lake already.

No, there had been no farewells from that quarter. He could have seen her when he came to collect Marcus yesterday. He could have sent a message enclosed in Mr van Meere's missive. He had to have known that his employer was writing to Millie. The two men had clearly talked over the prospect of a correspondence. And Dustin Seacombe had even confided to his employer that he had invited her and Millie to his own ranch.

Why, then, had there been no good-bye?

And why did it distress her so?

No, not distress. Irritate.

Georgia's sapphire walking skirts whipped around her ankles with the briskness of her stride.

Blasted man, making all sorts of hints and then leaving without a word. Well. She was no schoolgirl, to burst into tears because a boy had written his name on her dance card and then left the ball. She was a grown woman, and not without charm, if she said so herself. Any hints he had made had been the result of the danger they had shared, that was all. It was likely quite common, in those who led more exciting lives than she had before this trip.

By now *Foresight* would have left Europe astern and be embarking upon the Atlantic crossing. He would be thinking of home, and friends he had there. He would almost certainly not be thinking of her.

She must leave it at that and likewise strive to forget him.

CHAPTER THREE

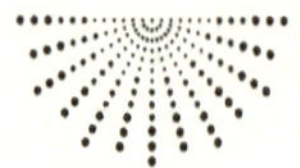

7:45 p.m.

They had just settled in the drawing room after an excellent dinner when they heard the peculiar *whoosh ... thump* of a tube arriving. Herr Brucker, Louise's butler, appeared a few minutes later with a note on a silver tray. It had been pressed flat, Millie noted, which seemed quite unnecessary given that the tube system was ubiquitous in large cities and everyone knew correspondence retained its rolled-up shape.

Louise scanned it rapidly, frowned, and handed it to Georgia, who read it together with Millie on the sofa.

May 13, 1895

Dear Lady Thorne,

We are pleased to be in receipt of your note requesting permission to call upon Landgräfin Winter with Lady Langford and Miss Brunel. I hope you will not find it presumptuous of myself and her household to express our condolences upon your recent loss.

I regret to say that her ladyship and Her Imperial Majesty's other ladies in waiting have been called away to wait upon the empress at Linderhof. They lifted yesterday morning. Her ladyship anticipated their return by Friday, which is, as you may remember, the day before the Maifest Ball. I am certain she will be delighted to see you during the festivities.

I remain, Madam, your obedient servant,

Dr P. Mainz, Master of the Household

Schloss Nymphenburg

Millie looked up to find Louise pacing in front of the fireplace. "I do not understand it," the latter said. "Does *wait upon the Empress* mean she is at Linderhof? Or that they are waiting for her to arrive? Oh, how I dislike ambiguity!"

"I cannot tell you." Georgia set the note upon the low table.

"It seems clear that to a lady in waiting, to *wait upon the empress* means to perform one's duties to her in person," Millie said. "Though what it means to the master of the household is a mystery, I agree."

"It is pointless to debate another's words," Louise said, "we will go and see for ourselves. If you agree, we will lift immediately after breakfast tomorrow."

"Why not tonight?" Georgia asked.

"Because, my dear, *Thetis* is in the hangar being repaired after her harrowing escape. They have promised me that she will be flightworthy tomorrow morning, not sooner."

"Oh." Color flooded Georgia's cheeks at this reminder that she had not only stolen a knight of the realm's personal vessel, she had managed to fly it into the path of a cannon-bomb as well. "I do hope the hull vane was not too badly damaged. And ... if it helps ... the empress assured me that since *Thetis* was damaged in service to the crown, she will foot the bill."

"I am sure she will—when we find her," Louise said. "For now, we must do our best to sleep, and be ready for what we discover."

"Louise—wait—" Millie stopped. Then she took a breath and rose from the sofa, feeling rather like an ensign giving bad news of the campaign to his general. "Two points to consider. One, you told the automaton today that you would not attend the ball because you were in mourning. And two, until the day before yesterday, your very life was in peril. Is it possible that you might leave these inquiries in Georgia's and my hands?"

With one swift look at her, Georgia stood also. "As a widow myself, my dear, I know there are matters one must deal with concerning estates and bequests. No one would blame you for concentrating upon—"

"I am not going to write replies to letters of condolence while the empress is missing!"

"It is a mournful business, I grant you. But Louise, consider. You are known wherever you go. Perhaps it would not be wise at this juncture to advertise it far and wide that you believe the empress to be the victim of some kind of plot. If Millie and I go to Linderhof and make quiet inquiries as to her situation, who will notice?"

"I can conjecture with some certainty that Herr Mainz has already sent a message to Countess Winter to tell her we wish to see her," Millie said. "It will seem normal for us to arrive, and normal to say that you declined to come for reasons of mourning."

Louise glared at them. "This rubs my fur the wrong way."

"It would mine, too," Georgia admitted. "But to those who have no reason to love either of us in Venice, I am presumed dead. I doubt Millie attracted their notice at all. *We* are not running the risk of … assassins."

Abruptly, Louise sat in the nearest armchair as though her knees had given out. "You believe there is a chance that villain Del Campo has—has called in the Famiglia Rosa? Has asked for one of the coins?"

Millie had no idea what that meant, but from Louise's loss of color, she suspected the Famiglia Rosa was one of the crime families she had heard talked of in whispers among the staff at their villa.

"I do not think it wise to risk it," Georgia went on. "Granted, they could attack you here, but you have a full staff to protect you. In the street—in the sky—" She left the obvious unsaid.

After a moment, their hostess nodded. "Very well. I will remain behind, and commence discreet inquiries of my own. Very discreet," she added hastily, as both Millie and Georgia opened their mouths to argue. "Promise me you will be equally discreet."

"I promise," Millie said.

Georgia only nodded. "We will send word as soon as we know anything."

Louise's color was coming back. "I wonder…" They waited for her to work through the idea that had just seemed to occur to her. "No, I cannot. Not after the fuss we had this morning."

Millie and Georgia exchanged a glance. It had been quite a morning. "With … Cora?" Georgia ventured. "Do you fear that she might also be a target?"

Louise frowned at the pattern in the carpet. "That wretch Del Campo has no qualms about using a child to get what he wants—he could have no qualms about killing one to make a point of his revenge."

"Oh, dear," Millie whispered. Must they fear his reach even here? "But you cannot live your lives under siege."

"No. But for a little while, would it be prudent to keep her in motion, at least until we know this present mystery is resolved? For all we know, Venice may already be exacting its revenge. They know we live here."

This was taking caution into the realms of nightmare, but Millie would not dream of saying so. "Are you suggesting that we take Cora with us tomorrow?"

"It would be as good as Christmas to that child," Georgia said dryly. "Being taken out of school and exercising a little spycraft—what more could an eleven-year-old want?"

"The thing is, Cora knows Linderhof as well as this house. She could be of use— No." Louise shook her head. "Her education is of greater importance than my fears."

"We have proven recently that fears are sometimes well founded," Millie said gently. "If you wish to risk the ire of her headmistress and entrust her to us, then I for one would be delighted. Goodness knows there is no one better suited to such an adventure—save yourself, and possibly Marcus Seacombe."

Louise gazed at them, clearly torn even though the idea had been her own.

Georgia took the matter in hand. "If you notify the Lycée tonight, we will collect her in the morning. We will return as soon as we know something. Possibly as soon as suppertime."

Louise rose and paced to the darkened windows and back,

rubbing her hands as though she were cold. "You're quite right. It is the errand of a day, no more. Sixty miles is less than an hour's flight."

On that comforting note, Millie said good night. It had been one of the strangest days of her experience, not counting, of course, their extraordinary stay in Venice.

Tuesday, May 14, 1895
8:00 a.m.

No one in the empire could have been happier or more excited to be released from lessons than Cora Thorne. Even her mother's worried eyes could not put a damper on her enthusiasm.

"I shall be as quiet as a mouse," she promised Georgia recklessly as Louise piloted the landau to *Thetis*'s moorage at the Theresienwiese airfield, where they had been notified the little vessel was flightworthy, supplied, and waiting for them, courtesy of the palace. "I'm quite used to sitting in parlors with fine ladies and not saying a word. They tend to forget I'm there, which is when it is most interesting."

Louise led them aboard. As Millie and Georgia stowed their valises in the tiny guest cabin with its two sleeping cupboards, and Cora's in her even tinier cabin, they heard Louise say, "My darling, now that we have some privacy, I must tell you the real situation." A rapid murmur followed.

Then came the sound of hands clapping in delight. "Mama! You do not say so—the empress has been replaced by her own automaton? Oh, this is thrilling. Mademoiselle will never be able to say my French essays are dull now, not when I have such a story."

"What kind of spy actually writes down her exploits?" Louise asked in scandalized tones.

Millie exchanged a twinkling look with Georgia. Now they should see how the scientist managed her offspring.

"No indeed, this is a matter of national importance," Louise went on. "I am sending you only because you know Linderhof so well, and your aunts—yes, we will maintain the convenient fiction that you are related—do not. You also have friends in the kitchen, don't you?"

"Yes," Cora said, "but Mama, you would not let me tell about the krakens and the underwater prison, either. Surely I can drop just a little hint? The girls in my form have heard me talk about the automaton before."

"No. This time, the empress's safety could depend on our discretion as we make our inquiries. Promise me, darling."

"All right," Cora said, though each syllable seemed to be drawn from her under protest.

Millie thought it prudent to make their appearance at this juncture. With a final hug, and a quite unnecessary admonition to be good and do as she was told, Louise descended the gangway to the grass. She took the time to inspect the newly repaired vanes herself while Georgia ignited the Daimler engines. Millie appreciated her nod of approval, which she could see through the viewing port from where she stood in the gondola.

When Georgia called, "Up ship!" the ground crew released the ropes and they fell up into the sky with a whoop from their small passenger.

"That's my favorite part," Cora said, waving as Louise shrank rapidly to the size of a thimble. "Oh, I'm so happy to be going along. I know I can help."

"I know you can, too, darling," Millie said from the navigation table. "Now, perhaps you might begin with me. I can read a map for a train or landau journey, but this chart has no roads, only land forms, elevations, and points of the compass. Where is the airfield that serves the royal palace?"

"It hasn't got one," Cora said. She put a finger on a small square labeled with the palace's name. "The village is way at the bottom of the mountain, five or six miles away. So everyone simply lands in the park. You have to be careful, though. The wind comes down the mountain and plays tricks on airships. Bounces them about like balloons."

Georgia came into the gondola just in time to hear. "What sort of tricks?"

"Mama says it's unpredictable. She always tells me not to talk when she's on approach."

"I shall adopt the same practice, then," Georgia said with a smile. "Though if we're about to hit something, I beg you will tell me."

"I'd tell the automaton intelligence system, rather," Cora objected. "It knows my voice. Yours, too, Auntie Georgia, if you flew her all the way from Venice."

"With a broken vane," Millie put in. "From the steam cannon on the Lido."

"Brilliant!"

Two days without the lovable Cora was simply two days too many. Millie made a note to herself to rescind her caution to Georgia about its being more important to go home. Teddy's arrival was two weeks away yet.

Between Georgia and the automaton intelligence system, they brought the vessel in with only a minor deviation, quickly corrected. Millie observed on the approach that three other vessels were also moored there—having conveyed the ladies in waiting, perhaps? A small ground crew caught the ropes and tied them to the mooring irons.

Cora disembarked at her usual run, heedless of possible slips on the gangway. "Who do these ships belong to, Emil?" she asked one of the young men, hardly more than a boy.

"Empress Christina's ladies," he said, confirming Millie's guess. "What a fuss and to-do getting them all off the ships and up to the castle. For of course they was too fine to walk."

They could see the castle from here. It couldn't be a quarter of a mile, on a lovely graveled path as straight as an arrow's flight.

"Luckily, we are not so fine," Georgia said. "Is the empress here, then?"

"Not that I know of," the boy told them. "They expect her any moment. They probably thought you was her—none of them knows a Zeppelin from a Meriwether, or sizes either. Empress Christina's ship, now. It's a beauty." His eyes took on a faraway gaze, as if he could see it in the sky. "If I could be a middy on *Sisi*, I would think I'd died and gone to heaven. She's a Zeppelin LZ-64, you know, with the latest model Daimler engines and an intelligence system so good you only need to *think* a change in course, practically, and she obeys you."

"She does sound a beauty," Georgia said with a smile. "I look forward to seeing her myself."

"Your captain can escort you for a tour. The empress doesn't mind."

"Lady Langford doesn't have a captain," Cora informed him, her nose wrinkling at such a thought. "She flew *Thetis* here herself, because Mama couldn't come. I helped navigate."

The boy looked at Georgia with new appreciation. "You

don't say, ma'am. The empress pilots her ship herself, too. She's the only one I know of, other than yourself now, and Cora's mum."

Millie thought it best not to share the information that many women in England could fly their own airships. Many Wit women, she amended. Blood women such as Georgia very rarely did—why, they were thought terribly racy if they drove a curricle and matched pair to town to look at hats.

She and Georgia had not brought court clothes in their valises, only a change of underthings, a nightdress, and a walking costume should their errand extend to more than a day.

"The ladies will have to receive us in flight clothes," Millie said airily, though feeling rather brave and daring to say so. "Surely they do not expect us to change to morning gowns simply to ask a few questions."

"If they do, I shall think as little of them as young Emil does," Georgia said. "I rather like my flight clothes."

She looked very well in the wool weskit with its double row of silver buttons and velvet facings, white blouse, and navy gabardine skirt. Millie was dressed in similar fashion, but her weskit was dark green, her skirt black. Their hats were similarly practical, being short of brim and low of crown to accommodate flight goggles, and trimmed only with grosgrain ribbon. Practical, unfussy clothing for a practical application, as Georgia would say.

Schloss Linderhof was a little jewel-box of a palace, the entirety of which could likely have fit within the bounds of the lake at Nymphenburg. "The old prince who lived here lived in a fairytale in his head," Cora confided as they mounted the fan of steps. "The empress took out all the awful furniture and turned his hall of mirrors into her workshop. There's still a lot of gold on the walls, but you can ignore it."

"We are here to see Landgräfin Winter," Georgia reminded her, "not to go prying into the empress's workshop."

"It's the most interesting part," Cora protested.

Georgia gave the butler her card, and presently they were shown into a room overflowing with ladies, busy with embroidery or playing cards. One enterprising individual was set up on the terrace outside, painting. This, it turned out, was the Landgräfin Winter.

"How talented you are, ma'am," Georgia said with some admiration after introductions concluded. "I am an indifferent painter, but clearly you possess true talent."

"Why, thank you." Her ladyship was a woman of some *avoirdupois*, but her touch with the brush was delicate and even Millie could see her use of color was expert. "I enjoy painting. There is always something to learn, isn't there?"

"For me, there is everything to learn," Millie said with a sigh. "I am merely a beginner, encouraged by Lady Langford, my niece by marriage."

The lady rinsed her brush and waved them over to a set of iron chairs set around a table. "Do you care for refreshment?"

"Thank you, but no," Georgia said. "We had hoped to see Her Imperial Majesty today in response to her summons, but the ground crew informs us she has not yet arrived."

"It is a bit of a puzzle as to why she hasn't, since we were advised yesterday she would need us here. I expected to find her in her workshop when we arrived. If she does not come today, I shall be quite dismayed, for I shall miss my grandson's birthday."

"A puzzle indeed," Georgia said. "We waited on her at

Nymphenburg and were told she was already here. Yet she requested specifically that we do so at the palace."

Millie thought it odd that Georgia did not mention the substitute in the audience chamber.

"Is that so." The countess looked troubled. "It is not like her to lose track of her schedule like that. She has a very orderly mind. Perhaps some matter came up that could not be delayed."

"If it had, surely you would have been informed," Millie offered.

"Not always. Though all her ladies in waiting have a copy of the schedule, sometimes it does change." She pulled a small, leather-bound folder from a drawer in her easel, and opened it. Under yesterday's date was a schedule written on a crested sheet of paper in a tiny but flawless copperplate hand. "Yes, here you are. *Lady Thorne and guests*. But we had already gone by then—I must confess, I thought you would be attending her here. Lady Thorne is in and out constantly." She smiled at Cora. "*Thetis* is so common a sight in the park that one thinks nothing of it."

"We are flying in her today, ma'am," Cora said shyly. "Lady Langford piloted her."

The countess's eyebrows rose as she returned her gaze to Georgia. "Did you? You are one of those avant-garde women like Louise, are you?"

"I would not say so," Georgia replied with a smile. "Just ask my son, Baron Langford. But I do enjoy it. And the flight here is so short I can see why Louise makes it so often. Though…" She paused delicately. "As she is in mourning, she will likely be less able to. Which is why we came today in her stead, to inquire after the empress's whereabouts. But I see you are as much in the dark as we."

"She must be at Nymphenburg," Countess Winter said firmly. "She is certainly not here."

"The closest we came to seeing her was her likeness—the automaton," Millie said, omitting the actual nature of that sighting. "What a very strange thing it is. I have never seen its like."

Countess Winter's face had drawn into a frown, as though someone had pulled strings. "That appalling creature. Strange, hmph! It is an abomination, and she loves it the way I used to love my dolls. But she is not a girl. She is a woman grown, and a head of state besides."

An abomination? An odd term, surely, for an inanimate object? "It seemed harmless enough," Millie said. "Isn't it?"

"Oh, I do not suppose it would murder us in our beds," the countess said with a sniff. "But there is nothing quite so disconcerting as to see a woman walking down the corridor and believe it to be one's royal lady, only to find out it is *that* uncanny thing." She shuddered. "The empty eyes, the toneless voice. I said abomination, and I meant it."

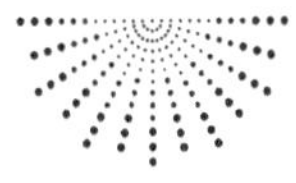

CHAPTER FOUR

*I*t cannot perambulate about stark naked," Georgia said, very much wanting to work up to her real question. "Its resemblance to Empress Christina would rule that out entirely, would it not?"

"Of course it doesn't," Countess Winter said. "It is dressed daily, like a doll, unless Her Imperial Majesty chooses to work on it."

"Oh, ma'am," Millie said. "It must be difficult for you, dressing the thing when you dislike it so."

She looked aghast. "My dear Miss Brunel, I do not dress it. Good heavens! If I were asked to, I should refuse. All my companions—" She waved in the direction of the open French doors, and the ladies within. "—know my feelings. No, someone else has that dubious pleasure."

"One of the others?" Georgia asked, cocking her head toward the doors.

"No indeed. That would be like asking us to work on a boiler, wouldn't it? No, if the empress doesn't dress it herself, one of her laboratory assistants does. It has a limited wardrobe, which simplifies such an unpleasant duty."

"Limited?" Georgia could not help a dreamy sigh. "When we saw it, it was wearing a cream silk receiving gown by Worth. What wouldn't I give to have a wardrobe limited to such glory!"

"What did you say?" The spine of the countess had gone absolutely rigid. "When did you see this?"

"Why, yesterday. When we waited upon her. Landgräfin, may we confide in you?"

"Yes. But about the gown—"

"It was wearing it in the audience chamber," Georgia said in a tone pitched low enough that even one of the ladies sitting nearest the door could not hear. "It—it *received* us, ma'am. It was not until we were in the private sitting room behind the throne, and giving our report of recent events in Venice, that Louise realized it was not the empress, but the automaton."

The countess appeared to have been deprived of speech. The knuckles of the hands still clutching the leather folder had gone white.

Millie ventured, "Is this the empress's normal practice? To delegate official duties to the automaton?"

"Could you fetch me some water?" the countess whispered. "There. In the room."

Cora leaped to her feet and sped off, and in a moment returned with a glass of water. The countess drained half of it.

"Will you be all right, ma'am?" Cora asked. "Would you like more?"

"Something sweet, I think," Georgia said when the lady did not speak. "To help the mind recover from the shock."

Cora was back in a moment with a small plate of candied fruit and marzipan almonds. The countess took some obediently and in a moment her color began to return. Cora took an almond, and Georgia thought it only polite to take a slice of candied orange, while Millie chose several blueberries coated in tiny crystals of sugar.

"I cannot believe it," the countess said at length. "This has never happened before."

"The strangest of all was that it did not appear as though *anyone* knew," Millie said, also keeping her voice low. "Even Count von Zeppelin behaved as if the empress were her normal human self."

The countess made a sound in her throat that somehow indicated derision. "That man is as enamored of mechanics as ever the empress could be. Even if he did realize it was not she, he would admire the likeness and applaud her for pulling the wool over everyone's eyes."

"You believe it to be a prank, then?" Georgia asked. "That Empress Christina dressed the automaton in one of her loveliest gowns and sent it out to impersonate herself?"

The countess shook her head. "During a requested audience with one of her intimate circle? My royal lady is many things, but rude and inconsiderate she is not. I cannot believe she would have done such a thing, and scampered off on some scheme of her own. She was incensed about the Doge's treatment of Lady Thorne." She took them both in as realization dawned in her eyes. "Is that why you are really here? For if she is not there and not here, then where is she?"

"Our questions exactly, ma'am," Georgia said with a nod. How refreshing it was to converse with a woman who could leap from *A* to *D* without needing endless explanations about *B* and *C*.

"Mama's, too," Cora said. "She sent us to ask them since she could not come. Because of Papa."

"Quite right." The countess touched Cora's hair, still braided from her brief stay at school, then cupped her cheek affectionately before she turned back to Georgia and Millie. "This must stay between the four of us. No one must know."

"I quite agree," Georgia said. "So you share our opinion that this is not normal, and it is not unreasonable or hysterical to believe that something might be amiss?"

"When it comes to heads of state, even something as innocent as a fly in the room where no flies should be can indicate something is amiss." The countess's tone was hushed. "This is far more than a fly. It also cannot go on for long. The substitution must soon be discovered. And then heaven help us all."

"We had thought that as Mistress of the Robes, you would be the one to discover it," Millie said. "I wonder if your being ordered here was merely a ruse to prevent such a discovery?"

"Who gave you the order?" Cora asked. "Empress Christina?"

One arched eyebrow rose. "You are as perceptive as your dear mama. Only one person may order me hither and yon, other than my dear Landgräf, who chooses his occasions wisely. I was given a note, signed by the empress."

Cora nodded, clearly thinking this over. "Can the automaton write?"

"No, thank goodness."

"Then perhaps it was forged. Even I could do a decent job of it, if I practiced."

"I hope you do practice your handwriting," Millie put in.

"It will be useful in what I predict will be an illustrious career."

"I am going to be a spy, ma'am," Cora confided to the countess. "Aunt Millie knows I am already practicing."

"So I see." The lines of strain in the woman's face were softening. "Perhaps you can find out who dressed the automaton yesterday, then, for it certainly was not any of us."

Cora looked delighted. "An assignment! Truly?"

"Which you will share with us," Georgia said before this got out of hand. "An excellent point, ma'am. We will do our best to find out." Although she was not just sure how it was to be managed. People didn't just waltz into Nymphenburg and ask the way to the empress's private chambers.

Millie leaned forward, her face alight with what was clearly a flash of inspiration. "Ma'am, perhaps we might carry an order of some kind from you. That would give us a pretext on which to enter the palace and make inquiries."

"Perhaps I should return and make them myself," the lady said thoughtfully. "For then I should be able to go to my grandson's birthday party this evening."

"Would it look suspicious if you were to come with us to Munich?" Georgia asked. "Forgive me—I have no knowledge of the duties of a lady in waiting. While we are traveling, I have not even a lady's maid. Millie and I help each other with buttons and hooks, and that is the extent of it."

"Consider yourself lucky," sighed the countess, who, Georgia had to admit, was dressed to the teeth in silk and ruffles and pearls, and it was only midmorning. "Yes, we come and go as we are needed. Even were the empress to turn up this afternoon, one of the other ladies could help her change for dinner. If you will give me but half an hour, I will accompany you."

"Millie and I will prepare for lift," Georgia said, rising with the countess.

"Is there time for me to visit Anya in the kitchen?" Cora asked hesitantly. "I only want to say hello, no more."

Georgia snapped open the chronometer on her lapel and leaned over to show her the time. "We lift at ten thirty."

"Thank you, ma'am." She turned and curtsied to the countess. "I won't be late." She ran down the terrace steps and vanished through a hedge, which Georgia could only assume led somehow to the kitchen garden.

"Is she really going to be a spy?" the countess said in a wondering tone, collecting her paint pans and putting away her brushes with sure movements. "At that age, I wanted to be a ballerina."

"She already is, ma'am," Millie said. "I daresay there are spies out there who have not a quarter of her experience."

10:27 a.m.

Cora ran up the gangway with three minutes of the allotted time to spare. The ground crew released the ropes and for the second time that morning, the deck pressed up under Georgia's boots and they fell upward into the sky. She had learned it was more graceful to simply bend one's knees until the vessel reached its sailing altitude. The ability to adapt even in such small matters was evidently not one of the countess's gifts, she found when she joined her in the saloon. She had remained firmly upon the sofa until the engines had begun to make way.

"I would offer you tea, but I am afraid the galley is rather empty yet," Georgia said apologetically.

The countess waved a hand. "I am in no need of it. I am so anxious about this matter that my stomach is in knots."

"Would you like a lozenge?" Cora pulled a purple hard candy from her pocket. "Anya gave me some of these. They are elderberry, and taste lovely."

"Thank you, dear." The countess was clearly used to children, for she popped the sweet in her mouth as though thoughts of pocket lint had never crossed her mind. "Delicious."

"The kitchen is in quite an uproar," Cora said, curling up in a corner of the sofa, which Georgia assumed was her particular place during voyages. "They didn't know you ladies were coming until you landed in the park yesterday. The cook was beside herself."

"I am sorry for that," the countess said, frowning. "It is unusual for the master of the royal residences not to let them know. And the dinner was excellent."

"That was because there was supposed to be some other meeting," Cora told her. "They'd got food in for a party of gentlemen. Do they eat different things than ladies?"

"They certainly *drink* different things," Millie observed.

"I did think the roast of venison was rather plainly dressed," the countess said thoughtfully. "No plum sauce, which the empress enjoys."

"A party of gentlemen expected, yet no notice of the ladies' arrival, to say nothing of the empress," Georgia said. "Do gentlemen tend to use the royal palaces if the empress is not in residence? Her ministers, perhaps?"

"No," the countess said bluntly. "If the Cabinet needs to

meet on some matter of secrecy, they certainly don't fly an hour south to a deserted house to do it. They've been known to meet in an underground room at Nymphenburg, and once to my knowledge at the home of the Minister of War during that dreadful affair with the *navires sous-marins* off the coast of France. No one at court would be so presumptuous."

What affair with undersea ships? But now did not seem the time to ask for details. She must attend to the matter at hand, which goodness knew was puzzling enough. "What about the heir?" Georgia asked. "Rupert von Mecklenburg? Could it have been he?"

"Certainly not. They are not his palaces. Yet. Perhaps they never will be, if my royal lady would only look about her for a husband worthy of her."

"I think the archduke could do it without telling her," Cora said. "Linderhof is nice, and Anya says the hunting is very good."

"If he did, he has violated the rules of protocol, to say nothing of good manners, in a dreadful fashion," the countess said. "Imagine ordering supplies for a dinner in a home that is not your own!"

"More than one dinner," Cora said, hunting in her pocket for the last sweet. "Two dinners, breakfasts and lunches, and some kind of party outside, Anya said. You should have heard Frau Berne. She's head cook. I learned a new swear word in German."

The Landgräfin Winter stared, but not because of bad language. "You cannot be serious. Who is this Anya, child, who gives you such information?"

"She's the cook's granddaughter. We've been friends since

Mama started going with the empress to Linderhof to work in her laboratory." Cora sucked on her sweet, apparently not much disturbed by the countess's dangerous tone. "It's lucky they did get all that in, otherwise you'd have been eating whatever they had on hand." She paused a moment to consider. "Mind you, what's on hand in a royal palace is probably very nice, too."

"I am finding all this very difficult to believe." The countess rose, clearly agitated. "I shall investigate the moment we arrive. Something is out of joint here, and of all things, that is what I most dislike."

Georgia couldn't help but agree. Small things—oddities—easy to overlook in themselves, but like straws, they indicated which way the wind was blowing. If there was a wind in evidence. It could all simply be a case of poor planning—someone or other being derelict in their duty. It could be a case of a royal lady wanting time to herself. But Georgia was not so sure. Straws … flies in the room …. If the Landgräfin Winter was this disturbed, it had to mean something.

Once they were moored, the airfield's landau conveyed them to Nymphenburg, where Georgia took the liberty of sending Louise a tube from the countess's suite of rooms.

L—

>*Our quarry was not there, and indeed was not expected until the ladies arrived yesterday. Conversely, a party of gentlemen was expected, but did not arrive. Mistress of the Robes knew nothing of the automaton and is appalled. Something murky is going on. She is with us at N., as is Cora. Useful child! Will return in time for dinner this evening to tell all.*

>*G.*

When the tube had whooshed away into the labyrinth that would take it to Kastanienhof within a few minutes, and the countess had refreshed herself and removed her hat, they set out along the palace corridors like hunters in search of prey.

"We might first determine where the automaton is and what it is doing," Millie suggested. "I should not like to run into it unawares, particularly if it is masquerading as the empress."

"I should like to pull its arms off, beat it with them, and bring this charade to an end," the countess said grimly, walking so fast she resembled an old-fashioned tea clipper under full sail.

"I beg you not to do that," Georgia said, fairly certain the lady would, given sufficient provocation. "If the court were to realize the empress is missing, it could precipitate a constitutional crisis."

"I am fully aware of that. I will restrain myself, never fear. The schedule this hour has her in the small ballroom giving out awards to graduating members of the Lycée des Jeunes Filles. We shall peek in from the rear."

The large room was filled to bursting with young ladies of seventeen and eighteen, their parents, younger classes, and members of the court. At the front, wearing a gown of spring green satin that set off the red diagonal sash bearing several medals indicating the various orders to which the empress belonged, the automaton was doing the honors. All unsuspecting, the young ladies advanced to the dais, curtseyed to the ground, and were awarded what appeared to be diplomas rolled up and tied with ribbon.

The countess said something in German between her teeth that made Cora look up at her with admiration. "Come," the former said hastily. "This will go on for another half hour at least. I will find who is dressing that thing if it is the last thing I do. The Order of the Crown of Prussia, on that abomination's breast!"

"It doesn't have breasts." Cora practically had to run to keep up.

"Hence the high necklines, I suppose," Millie said breathlessly. "Cora, one does not speak of body parts in public."

"Even if we're talking about the automaton? It isn't human. Why may its parts not be spoken of?"

"They may, certainly," Georgia said, striking out into the depths in response to Millie's speaking glance. "But in private. And in these circumstances, not at all. Since no one knows, as we do, that it is performing in there."

Cora seemed to accept this as reasonable, and once they arrived in the empress's private apartments, curiosity kept her quiet.

The countess led them straight to the empress's dressing rooms, of which there were three. "Day dresses and informal attire such as she wears in the laboratory," she said as she passed the first archway, "State gowns and diadems, and dinner and evening gowns and jewelry." She led them through the third archway. "Halt, you!"

Georgia's stride faltered until she realized that their guide was speaking to someone in a vast closet stuffed with gowns such as she had never dreamed of. Most of the garments were enclosed in silk envelopes, and a young woman stood next to a table at one end, where she was in the process of enclosing a cream gown in a similar envelope.

Oh, let it be the Worth, that I may see it up close!

To her disappointment, the side had been buttoned closed

by the time they caught up. "Landgräfin," the girl said, and sank to the floor in a curtsey.

"Do get up. Ingrid, isn't it?"

"Yes, ma'am." She rose. "This one was not soiled at all. I sent it downstairs, but they could find nothing to do, so they sent it back."

"Did you dress Her Imperial Majesty yesterday?"

The girl gaped at her as though she were mad. "I, ma'am? Certainly not. You did."

"I was at Linderhof, waiting upon her. Who did, if you did not and I did not?"

"I—why—" She stammered to a halt. "If it was not you, ma'am, then I do not know."

"Who dressed her in the apple green this morning, Ingrid?" Millie asked gently. The girl looked as though she were about to burst into tears. "With the royal orders?"

"I do not know that, either. I was told to fetch back the Worth, so I did."

"By whom?" the countess demanded.

"Forgive me, ma'am, but I thought she was the new lady in waiting. I did not recognize her, and she did not introduce herself."

"Can you describe her?" Georgia asked. "Tall—short—blond—bald?"

"Not bald, ma'am." Poor Ingrid must be of a very literal turn of mind. "Tall, about my height. Blond like me, but her hair was up under a cap like this, so I couldn't see much of it." She touched the lace cap that covered her own hair.

In other words, someone who would be mistaken for this young woman at a distance, and no questions asked. Then again, Georgia thought, trying to be fair, there were any number of tall, blond young women in Bavaria. Half the graduates in the ballroom just now fit that description.

"Thank you, Ingrid," the countess said. "You may return to your duties."

The young woman curtsied again, and took up the Worth with appropriate reverence to return it to its place on the rail.

"So we are no closer to the truth than when we arrived," Georgia murmured to Millie as they made their way past the dressing rooms. Catching movement in the one that held the evening gowns, she said in some alarm, "Cora, darling, please do not touch anything."

"But it's lovely." The girl hovered over an open drawer in a sideboard that featured two dozen such drawers. "Come look." A pearl and emerald necklace lay in a depression in the velvet that fit it exactly. "It looks like it is made of snowdrops."

That it did, and was so beautiful Georgia had to tell herself, *Thou shalt not covet thy neighbor's jewelry.* "In future, Cora, please remember that one does not rummage about in drawers belonging to other people. Particularly royal people."

"This necklace goes with the dress in which—" The countess dropped her voice to a whisper. "—that *thing* is dressed this morning." She slid the drawer closed. "Whoever dressed it did not know that. I find it deeply disturbing that anyone but members of my staff are at large in my royal lady's private chambers."

It *was* deeply disturbing. "It also shows a fine talent for misdirection and guile," Millie pointed out. "And for organization. Imagine the planning needed to carry off such a deception."

"There are too many moving parts for it to go on for long,"

Georgia said. "Landgräfin, what did Ingrid mean, 'the new lady in waiting'?"

"I should like to know that myself." She pulled a fine chain from under her bodice. From it hung two small keys. With one, she locked the long jewelry cabinet, and with the other, she checked a similar cabinet in the closet. It was locked already. "It is obviously a ruse should anyone question this person—Her Imperial Majesty has not appointed another."

"How many of you are there?" Millie asked.

"Ten—one from each of the medieval land-owning families." She paused. "Well, nine at the moment. Baroness Salzmann is in a delicate condition, and is awaiting her confinement at their estate a little east of Salzburg."

"Then I should like to volunteer to take her place," Millie said promptly, "and become a new lady in waiting myself."

CHAPTER FIVE

KASTANIENHOF

Tuesday, May 14, 1895
8:00 p.m.

hat did she say to that?" Louise Thorne paused in the act of spearing a stem of white asparagus, which was in season and quite the most delicious vegetable Millie had ever tasted.

"After she recovered from my audacity in suggesting it," Millie said, "she quite warmed to the idea. With all the ladies in waiting at Linderhof, *someone* is instructing the maids and dressing the automaton. She will attend her grandson's birthday party this evening, and return to Linderhof in the morning as though nothing is wrong. Georgia and I, meanwhile, have *carte blanche* to investigate."

"Auntie Georgia and the Margravine von Karlsrühe, you mean," Cora corrected her with her usual attention to detail.

"Heavens," Louise said. "Are you to impersonate that lady, Millie? For I assume you know she is a real person."

"I am and I do," Millie said. "The countess assures me she

is at the other end of the country, and hardly ever leaves her lands. I am to play the margravine, who is about my age, newly come to court and therefore quite clumsy and inexperienced. One might even say dotty and distracted. The sort of person with whom one might let one's guard down. Oh, and Landgräfin Winter is lending me Baroness Salzmann's suite of rooms."

"She won't like that," Louise said with a smile tinged just slightly with anticipation. "Emma Salzmann is the youngest and most recent addition to the empress's ladies in waiting, and quite the most high and mighty about her elevation at court."

"By the time she recovers and wants her rooms back, we shall have found the empress," Georgia said. "The countess mentioned she is in a delicate condition—is that really so?"

"She is three or four months along, I think." Louise dipped a piece of asparagus in its sauce and savored it. "You will immediately forget I said this, but it is my opinion she was enjoying the archduke's parties in the lodge a little too much for Landgräfin Winter's liking. It is entirely possible she was sent home to cool her heels in an effort to discipline her spirits."

"Whatever the reason, her absence is convenient. It will enable Millie to discover what is going on in the palace." Georgia turned her attention to her pork medallions in currant sauce, her wild rice and, of course, her asparagus.

"And what are you going to do while Millie is occupied there?" Louise asked.

"Auntie Georgia has no friends in the kitchens," Cora observed. "Nor do I, or I might help."

"You, my darling spy, must return to the Lycée in the morning," her mother informed her.

"Mamaaaaa."

"Your mama is quite right," Georgia said in a serious tone. "You are already recognizable here in Munich because of her friendship with the empress. If you are to remain useful, you must not be too much in evidence too often. We do not want the wrong people asking questions."

"Oh." Cora looked as though this had never occurred to her before. "But if I can be useful, you'll tell me, won't you? You won't leave me out while you have all the fun?"

"Certainly not," Millie said. "We of all people know not to risk the success of our endeavors by doing *that.*"

Gratified, Cora took another helping of asparagus.

Georgia, Millie noticed, had not answered Louise's question. She did not do so until Cora had gone to bed and they had retired to the drawing room with small glasses of tawny port.

Louise wasted no time. "So, my dear, what *will* you be doing while Millie is swanning about in the palace? For that matter, what will I be doing? For I feel rather like Cora—I do not wish to be put out to grass simply because of the conventions of mourning." She gazed at the wedding portrait over the fireplace mantel. "I should take that down and replace it with the Sisley in the foyer. Am I horrible for not mourning Francis?"

There was only one person whose experience in marriage might give her the right to advise a new widow. Millie took a sip of her excellent port and waited.

"I agree that it is impossible to mourn the man who died," Georgia said slowly. "So no, you are not horrible. You are a woman who has been betrayed in one of the many ways a woman can be betrayed by the one she once loved."

"You sound as though you know."

In halting sentences, Georgia gave the barest outlines of what had happened to an innocent eighteen-year-old bride during the years of her marriage to Hartford Brunel. Even the outlines made Louise's face lose its color.

"I was only able to overcome the rage and the betrayal enough to put on weeds if I mourned the man I thought I loved. He was a phantom—a fiction of my own inexperienced heart—but imagining that man in the coffin being lowered into the ground enabled me to shed healing tears." Georgia paused. "It was a beginning. Teddy's coming into his inheritance and charting his own course in life healed my heart far more. And I would have gone through worse if I knew I should have Teddy in the end."

Millie thought she might safely speak at this juncture. Certainly not a word of what she had been through with Georgia—and alone, at her nephew Hartford's hands—would ever cross her lips. "It was Teddy who launched us upon this venture," she explained quietly. "He felt that seeing a little of the world would bring his mother out of herself, and give her happier memories to reflect upon."

"In that he was right." Georgia smiled, her eyes soft as she thought of her son. "I am looking forward to telling him about the krakens." Her gaze returned to Louise. "Guilt is an unproductive emotion. If you must break china and scream your rage to the heavens, do so. We will not blame you. If you cannot mourn the diplomat who took your daughter to Venice, then mourn the man in that wedding portrait, who smiles as though his dearest wish has been granted. In the end, I hope you feel the same gratitude for your child as I do for mine. For without the man, we would not be provided for, and we would not be able to safely bring up the children we love more than our own lives."

Silence fell as Louise reflected on what she had heard. After a few minutes, she said, "Thank you. I know it cost you to share your experience with me."

"It was a cost I was willing to pay. Friendship, you see, is more dear to me than any misplaced notions of pride or shame."

"You have nothing to be ashamed of," burst from Millie in a stifled whisper before she could prevent it. Shame was for people who had betrayed themselves and the people who loved them. For people who destroyed love in the name of selfishness.

Georgia reached across the sofa cushion and squeezed her hand. "Not in the matters we have been talking of, perhaps. And there have been many nights when the only thing I had to be thankful for was your love. It saw me through."

Millie would not cry. So undignified. She gave a mighty sniff and squeezed Georgia's fingers in return.

"I must turn from the past for the moment, and consider the future, or I shall be the one in tears," Louise said, her voice husky. "May we once again take up the subject of my missing friend?"

"We may," Georgia said. "Landgräfin Winter is our bulwark against discovery. Millie is stationed in the empress's private rooms, to gather as much information as she can. You and I …" She paused. "Honestly, Louise, I am at a loss. I know so little of Munich, and absolutely nothing of the empress's habits or life at court. Where do we even begin?"

"What would Mr Holmes do?" Millie prompted.

Even Louise smiled, and her tears abated entirely. "He would ask, who has the most to gain by her disappearance?"

"Do you read Sir Arthur Conan Doyle's works, too?" Georgia looked intrigued.

"No, but Cora does, and regales me with his ingenious solutions. She considers his books research, you know. So to answer our friend the detective, I would have to say Archduke Rupert must head the list."

"Agreed," Georgia said. "So we must beard him in his den and find out if he is involved."

"There is the Maifest Ball on Saturday," Louise mused. "He and all his cronies would never miss it—if only for the spread, which is legendary."

"Then we three will attend, mourning or no mourning," Georgia said firmly. "How well do you know him?"

"Well enough to despise him," she said shortly. "He is nearly forty and behaves like a schoolboy of seventeen. If Christina was meant to be an engineer, he was meant to be the kind of country squire whose only concerns are killing every animal on his acres and serving them up to his friends, while begetting children on his buxom bride whenever it suits him."

"He is married?" Millie said in some surprise.

"No, but there is no shortage of ladies vying for the privilege." Louise made a face. "I suppose someone may eventually put up with him for the honor of being an archduchess—and possibly an empress one day."

"Has he a mistress?" Georgia asked coolly.

Millie controlled a squeak of shock with difficulty.

"Not at the moment," Louise said. "Leaving the Baroness

Salzmann to rumor, I shall stick to facts. He was the protector of an opera singer, but she left to go on a tour to the Fifteen Colonies last autumn. I really think he prefers the company of men. What self-respecting woman would put up with him if *that* retinue were always underfoot?"

Georgia's face had taken on a calculating expression. "Will you introduce me?"

"Certainly, if you want—oh, Georgia, no. Absolutely not. I forbid it."

"What better way to get close enough to discover if he is involved?" Georgia sounded so reasonable it was all Millie could do not to demand of her what Teddy might think of this. Heaven forbid it got into the papers and he found out!

"For heaven's sake, we might simply ask him." Louise was beginning to look alarmed. "Tell me you are joking."

"I am not. If I can remove his attention from food and hunting for only a day or two—enough for a thorough look around that hunting lodge of his—then I am willing to make the sacrifice of taste and intelligence."

"But not, I trust, your reputation." Louise covered her face with her hands. "What have I done?" she groaned.

"The question is, what may you do yet?" Georgia said briskly. "You are too well known to be seen asking questions publicly. Tell me, is it possible to spirit the automaton out of the palace?"

Louise lowered her hands. "No indeed. That would cause the crisis we have been trying to avoid. Why would I want to spirit it anywhere?"

"You told us it remembers what is said. I would very much like to know what it heard between my begging the real empress for help on Saturday and our audience with it on

Monday. Could you extract its memories? Perhaps in Millie's borrowed rooms? No one would question the empress's visiting her newest lady in waiting."

Millie could see the moment when Louise's lively brain engaged with the possibilities this presented. "That is a very good idea. I am ashamed I did not think of it myself."

"You have had other matters on your mind," Millie reminded her. Grief did strange things to one's thinking without its being mixed with anger at the deceased. Marvel rather that Louise was still rational enough to join them in their inquiries.

"If the automaton comes to you, Millie, all I need do is access the panel in its back," Louise mused. "It is used to my tinkering with it, so it should not object."

Millie wondered how an inanimate object could object to anything.

"Excellent. I do like a plan, the simpler the better," Georgia said. "And if our three linked inquiries net us nothing, we will simply trim our sails and try another tack."

"Agreed." Louise rose. "Let us toast our enterprise with another glass of port. But I warn you, this must be the last. This vintage will lay you out faster than the archduke himself."

Wednesday, May 15, 1895
Nymphenburg, 10:00 a.m.

Before she returned to Linderhof to await a royal lady who would not arrive, the Landgräfin Winter introduced Millie to the Master of the Household, who saw to the needs of the ladies in waiting.

"It makes no sense for the margravine to make the trip to Linderhof when she might instead acquaint herself with the royal apartments, the grounds, the staff, and our routines here," she told Herr Doktor Mainz. "I know I leave her in safe hands."

"Thank you, Landgräfin. An airship is waiting to convey you back to Linderhof." With a smile, he turned to Millie. "It is an honor to have you with us, Margravine. If you would follow me, I will show you to your rooms. With the short notice, Baroness Salzmann's things are still being moved, but at least you will know the way there."

Millie did not mind getting a look at the young baroness's things, which might yield a clue as to what had gone on in the archduke's company. Her suite looked much like that of the Landgräfin Winter, as far as elegance, walls, and carpets went. But the senior lady's suite had been homelike, full of pictures and her paintings and a lovely Broadwood grand piano by the French doors looking out on the gardens. The baroness, on the other hand, was clearly not a woman who brought her tastes and pursuits with her wherever she went. The walls were the same blue and white panels as the Landgräfin's but bare of pictures, the furniture good but not outstanding, and there was no evidence of any pursuit except in the bedroom, where the dressing-table overflowed with pots of rouge, jewelry, a feather boa, and so many cards and invitations that they had to be piled in a basket.

A maid was in the process of clearing it all away and packing it in a fabric-sided box, presumably to go into storage until the lady's return. Likewise the closets were being emptied by another maid. Millie caught glimpses of more ruffles and lace than she had ever thought possible, to say nothing of kid opera gloves and enough feathered head-dresses and hats to refledge an entire flock of birds.

Millie's own brass-banded traveling closet waited by the door, her valise and a hatbox on top of it.

"I trust your luggage will arrive by train?" Dr Mainz inquired.

"No indeed," Millie said. "I do not possess much in the way of a wardrobe. There is no need for it in Karlsrühe."

"Then permit me to draw up a list of the apparel you will need in Her Imperial Majesty's service," he said with a bow. "Even if you are only with us until the baroness returns, at the very least, we must have a court gown, a ballgown and dinner gown for each night of the week, and the accoutrements that go with them. Did you bring a tiara or parures? Each suite has a locking box set into the wall."

Millie considered herself wealthy in the possession of the diamond brooch that had belonged to her mother.

"No, I left them at home." She flushed. "I did not think it prudent to travel with things of such value. I came on the train, you know. I do not care for these newfangled airships."

He paused. Airships had been in non-military use for half a century. "We will send for them, then."

"Oh, I beg you will not," she said hastily. "At least, not yet. You see, if I have them here, then my daughter—" *Please let the real margravine have a daughter.* "—will not be able to entertain suitably in my place."

He gazed at her. "Margravine, forgive me, but you must have a tiara for formal occasions when you attend the empress. It is unthinkable for you to be bareheaded during affairs of state."

She would ask to borrow Georgia's without delay.

"Very well. I will send for them."

"I can do that for you."

"No indeed. In the absence of the empress, I expect I have the time to rectify my own mistakes."

To her vast relief, he inclined his head in acquiescence. As for the ballgowns and dinner gowns, until she and Georgia located the empress they would find her so distracted and difficult to schedule for measurements and fittings that with any luck they would give it up.

With an air of moving on, Herr Mainz guided her into the sitting room and plucked from an inner pocket of his morning coat a leather folder similar to the one the countess carried. "Here is the empress's schedule. You will be introduced to her this afternoon, when she requests that you join her in her private apartments. Are you familiar with their location?"

"Yes, the Landgräfin showed me about, and told me what my duties would be. She is a very … how shall I put it? A woman of great authority."

"That she is, and glad we are for it. Please familiarize yourself with Her Imperial Majesty's engagements. Tomorrow morning, you will attend her to the Museum of Natural History, where she is opening a new wing."

"Shall I need a tiara?" Millie asked anxiously.

He smiled, as though she were Cora's age. She could almost hear him thinking, *How do they raise their ladies out there in the wilds of Karlsrühe that they do not know these things?* "No indeed, ma'am. Not for a morning engagement. A smart hat will suffice. I trust you are supplied with those?"

"Yes, I am." Her relief was an act. Mostly.

He bowed. "Perhaps you would care for a walk in the

gardens until these rooms are ready?" He indicated the French doors, bowed, and departed.

The gardens were lovely, but not useful for her purposes. Millie wasted no time in returning to the closets and the maids. In her dotty grandmother persona, she soon put them at ease, and while the one who made her escape first had a bad habit of rolling her eyes—and good riddance to her—the other seemed kind enough to have had a dotty grandmother of her own.

"What a lot of dresses the baroness has," Millie said. "Do let me help you with these. Are they all to go in these silk sleeves?"

"Yes ma'am. And you mustn't help. If Dr Mainz caught me allowing it, he would be so angry."

Millie sniffed at the idea. "So I am to dawdle in the hedges while you spend the entire day in the closet? I think not. If we get this done together, we can go outside and enjoy the day."

"Ma'am, I would be sacked if I dawdled in hedges."

"But you're my maid, aren't you? You can't be sacked if I ask you to show me about."

"No," the girl said hesitantly. "But it would seem awfully odd. Dr Mainz or another of the ladies usually does it for newcomers."

Millie lifted a green satin ballgown with a neckline so low it was a wonder the baroness didn't fall out of it. In moments she and the maid, whose name was Lisabet, had buttoned it into its sleeve and were on to the next one.

"The other ladies are at Linderhof waiting on the empress, and Dr Mainz is doing something more useful," Millie said cheerfully. "Is it a bit odd, all the ladies in one place and the empress in another?"

"It is, a bit, but it does happen if there is an engagement she cannot get out of."

"Like opening a wing of a museum?"

Now Lisabet rolled her eyes, but at least it wasn't at Millie's expense. "The archduke—the heir, you know—could probably do that. Though it would be funny. I don't think he has ever looked at a picture of anything but horses and antlers in his life."

"I heard he was a sportsman," Millie allowed. "Is he a handsome man?"

"I suppose some would think so." Her gaze flickered to the dressing table, now bare of the baroness's things except for some spilled powder and some dropped feathers from the boa.

"The baroness does?"

The girl's lips closed and she buttoned the next dress into its sleeve in silence.

"Oh, come, Lisabet. I am not one of your fancy court ladies. I have only just arrived in Munich and already I have heard speculation about the circumstances of her departure. She is in a delicate condition?"

Her lashes lifted. "Promise you won't tell where you heard it."

"I promise. I don't know anyone here to tell."

Lisabet whispered, "They say she's expecting his baby, and the baron, you know, is much older than she is. Apparently the poor man is over the moon about it. She's his third wife, and no children yet to inherit."

"She must have been quite far along when she went home, then?"

"She only came four months ago, and we think she's

about that far along. We won't be seeing her back here before the autumn, ma'am, so you should make yourself comfortable."

Millie shook her head, not at being comfortable, but at the coils people got themselves into. "Poor Baron Salzmann."

"Imagine the whole palace knowing, and him not."

Millie *tsk*ed. "I give you my word that you will not have to pack up *my* things for such a reason."

Lisabet burst into giggles, then clapped a hand to her mouth. "I'm so sorry, Margravine."

Millie twinkled at her. "I'm glad you have a sense of humor. My daughter despairs of mine. She thinks I do not live up to my title sufficiently."

At which point Millie was obliged to answer questions about her fictional daughter, who bore a strong resemblance to Georgia. Well, if a woman were to design a daughter for herself, Georgia would answer in almost every point. Millie had never understood how Mrs Montgomery, Georgia's mother, could estrange herself from her own child for the sake of Millie's beastly nephew, Hartford Brunel.

"Which reminds me, I must send for my jewels," she said to bring the topic to a graceful close. "Are we supplied with pen and paper?"

She was shown a neat little desk with stationery, ink, pens, and a communications cabinet close by. While Lisabet returned to the last of the packing, Millie wrote a note.

Dearest,

I am settling into the baroness's rooms and have been informed I must have a tiara at the very least, and a parure preferred. Do you have anything on hand that would do? I cannot imagine myself in the sapphires. I will fasten a necklace around my head and call it a tiara before I put those on.

I must also strategize several ways in which to avoid having ballgowns made. Seven of them, no less, and dinner dresses for each night of the week. Imagine the furor were the bills to arrive at Karlsrühe!

In haste—

M.

She reached into the desk drawer for an envelope, and her fingers encountered what felt like loose feathers. Or leaves. She pulled them out to find a sheet of similar stationery, torn into quarters. Civility dictated Millie should throw someone else's correspondence into the fire without reading it. But civility would not discover what was going on in this palace.

Millie lined up the pieces to form a note in a loopy feminine hand, the ends of words terminating in self-conscious flourishes.

Who are you to order me about in this way? Might I remind you that all depends on me, including your life? But go, take to your burrow and hide in the dark with the others. I am no coward. We proceed as if the

The note was unfinished. As though the author had been interrupted, and had torn it up and flung it in the drawer to prevent discovery.

Millie took the bottom left quarter into the closet. "Lisabet, do you recognize this handwriting?"

The girl glanced at the fragment, her arms full of russet-gold taffeta. "That's the baroness's hand, ma'am. I'm sorry if the housemaid hasn't had a chance yet to tidy up drawers and things. Your rooms will be perfect by the time you come back to dress for dinner, I promise."

Dress for dinner? Perhaps she had better have a look at that schedule. She had been hoping for a tray in her room.

After sending her missive to Kastanienhof, Millie tucked Baroness Salzmann's note into her pocketbook to show Georgia and Louise at the earliest opportunity. It sounded rather as if the young woman's activity at the palace might include more than simply sacrificing her virtue to the heir to the throne.

CHAPTER SIX

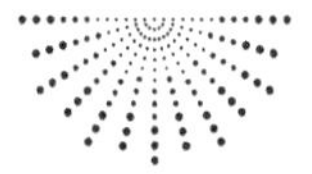

KASTANIENHOF

11:30 a.m.

With two and a half days before the Maifest Ball and an introduction to Archduke Rupert, Georgia began the hunt with a little research on her quarry.

Louise spread a selection of newspapers for her perusal on the low table in the sitting room, then departed for her laboratory. "I think better when I do something with my hands. I will go over every moment I was last with Christina, to see if any clue as to her state of mind or her whereabouts comes to mind."

Supplied with the delicious coffee Louise enjoyed of a morning, as well as warm croissants delightfully stuffed with bits of chocolate, Georgia lost herself in article after article about the archduke. What a good thing she enjoyed languages, and could read German as easily as the Queen's English! The court circular gave the archduke's schedule of appearances, amounting to about one-third of the empress's engagements. However, the substance of them was quite different.

Not for him the opening of museum wings, the encouragement of graduating students, or the giving of speeches in Parliament. No, here he was at the race track, firing the pistol for the opening race of the season, which had been a few days before. He had appeared at four society balls last week, always in the company of his group of friends—to the delight of their hostesses, no doubt, who would never turn down extra men. And here he was cutting the ribbon at the opening of a brewery, and having the spring batch named after him.

Here was an anomaly, however.

Georgia peered at the article in *The Scientific Review*, a publication that clearly disdained the engravings, daguerreotypes, and editorial cartoons of the society pages (the latter liberally sprinkled with likenesses of Rupert, some not so flattering). It seemed Rupert had attended a meeting of the Technical Philosophical Society, whatever that was. Georgia scanned the neat columns. Oh. He was bestowing a medal on someone for their service, and from the tone of the piece, they hadn't been altogether happy at the last-minute substitution of archduke for empress, due to some illness on the part of the latter. Georgia amused herself imagining the engineers' expressions at the inability of the archduke to have any conversation at all with them. Though that, of course, was not reported in the article.

She moved back to the court circular. The archduke was to unveil a new model of airship at the Zeppelin Airship Works on—she checked the date—goodness, this very afternoon. Excitement bubbled up inside her. She dropped the paper and hurried into the wing that housed Louise's laboratory.

"Yes, go by all means," Louise said absently, measuring chemicals into a flask. "You won't be able to get near him, but you might enjoy the airship works. Some of the civilian models are so lovely they make me want to spend Cora's tuition on one of them."

The days of Georgia's needing to be chaperoned about town were long over. She rather reveled in her freedom to simply hop on the open tram Louise had specified, and be carried across town to her destination as easily as one might use the London Underground. She had dressed carefully, with rather more froufrou to her blouse and one less petticoat under the skirts of her walking costume, and a pair of rather fetching drop earrings. A darling hat with a feather sat on curls she had dressed high, poufing out over her forehead and drawing attention to her eyes.

Though it had been twenty years since she had gone to such trouble, the hunter would become the hunted if she could only get near enough.

The Zeppelin Airship Works was dressed as if for a holiday, with bunting in the Bavarian colors of blue and white, a brass band playing mightily on the lawn, and a series of long tables laid out with refreshments under white tents. She followed the stream of people inside one of the vast hangars.

The archduke, it appeared, was not yet here, but the founder of the works certainly was, conversing with a small crowd that included his wife.

Perfect. Georgia made her way toward the well-dressed group and with no effort at all, caught Count von Zeppelin's eye.

His face lit up in a smile, and he beckoned her over. "My dear Lady Langford, what a pleasure to see you! May I have the honor of introducing my wife, Isabella?"

Georgia curtsied to the woman next to him. "The honor is mine, Gräfin. How do you do?"

The wife of one of the most famous men in the world was rather plain, with dark hair piled up under a tiny hat, and eyes that told Georgia she might be uncomfortable in crowds. "I am very well—the count has told me that he saw you at court with Lady Thorne on Monday. Are you enjoying your visit to Munich?"

"Very much," Georgia said, "not least because it is not Venice. Now, there is a country that is all beauty on the outside, and all danger within."

A smile broke out on the lady's lips that she tried to control, but failed. "I know one or two people who might fit that description, as well."

Georgia caught sight of a commotion in the massive open space of the doors. "Ah, here is your royal guest. I will not keep you."

"On the contrary, Lady Langford, I beg you will join our party. I am, as you see, the only female here, and I should enjoy your company. I fear the only reason I came with my husband is because I want so badly to see inside the ship he has been talking about for months. It is a civilian model, you know, and quite advanced."

Georgia accepted with only the briefest show of reluctance. Such luck!

The archduke and his retinue made the crowd part like the Red Sea, amid cheers and catcalls—depending, she supposed, on whether the person thought him fit for the crown or not. When she was introduced, she sank to the floor in a curtsey. When she rose, it was to find the royal gaze sliding down her figure with as much attention as she had given it this afternoon in her room.

"I am honored to meet you, Your Grace," she breathed, affecting to look up at him through her eyelashes, though she was nearly as tall as he.

"And I you, Lady Langford. Is your husband with you?"

He got right to the point, didn't he? "I am a widow, Your Grace. I am staying at present with Lady Louise Thorne, a dear friend."

"The prickly Lady Thorne," he said, and the gentlemen with him laughed. "A woman of such intelligence she terrifies me. Cut from the same cloth as von Zeppelin here, to say nothing of my cousin. Well, Count, I am agog to see this new ship of yours. Let's have that ribbon out of the way, and get a look at it."

Without asking permission, he tucked Georgia's hand into the crook of his elbow, obliging her to sail away with him across the expanse of the hangar floor, obliging her hosts, the Graf and Gräfin von Zeppelin, to follow them to the ship. The flash of portable daguerreotype cameras dazzled her eyes and she had a sinking feeling that her face was about to be on the front page of tomorrow's papers. It was a relief to climb the gangway of the ship and enter the relative calm inside.

The archduke was soon absorbed in the ship's beauties—its advanced automaton intelligence system, its elegant fittings in saloon and staterooms, its sailing speed and engine power. She slipped away to rejoin the countess with a sense of relief.

"Do let us have a look at the staterooms, Gräfin," she said. "If one is to fly great distances, I understand the comfort of one's sleeping cupboard can make a great difference."

"Do you travel much, Lady Langford?"

"Not before this trip, I am afraid. But now that my year of mourning is ended, my son insists that I go where I like and see the world's marvels, so here I am."

"My condolences on the one, and my congratulations on the other," the countess said. "How clever of you to have brought up such a generous young man!"

Laughing, they entered the first stateroom, admiring its soft carpets, its brass lamps, and the clarity of its viewing ports. The bed was indeed comfortable—as much as her own bed at home. And the luscious but restrained curves of the cupboard's Art Nouveau design made them both sigh with longing.

"I must do my duty," the countess confided when they had peeked into all four staterooms and the engine room. "We are to offer His Grace tea aboard, to demonstrate the capability of the galley. One person may operate the entire kitchen, can you believe it?"

"And that one person is to be you?"

The countess smiled her agreement, and hurried away to begin her preparations. Georgia ought to return to the archduke's orbit, but she couldn't help popping into the gondola first, just to have a look.

If the galley had been designed to be operated by one person, it followed that the gondola would be, too. She walked about the daring new design, which was tucked up into the very fuselage rather than hanging below it with stairs and ladders for the crew. She marveled at the simple changes that allowed control—most of the equipment could be moved closer on telescoping arms or trapezes to suit the reach of a single pilot. They shared their graceful, organic Art Nouveau design with the staterooms—as much art as engineering.

In addition, the company had clearly realized that England was far ahead of Europe in its support of civilian travel. Georgia was aware that any civilian ship might be seconded to the War Office's use should the country come under threat. An operating standby fleet of vessels like these was only to its advantage.

If she were to own such a vessel, she would need to be more than self-trained. What an exciting thought—to be as good at flying as any military pilot! What would that be like? And what would Teddy say?

"I should very much like to know what it is that makes you smile like that."

She turned from the viewing port to find the archduke stepping off the two cast-iron steps shaped like lily pads into the gondola. She had been thoughtless, leaving herself open in solitude like this. Her best option was the truth.

"The prospect of proper flight training should I one day own a vessel like this," she said gaily.

He stared, temporarily distracted from whatever urge had made him evade his hosts so completely in order to hunt her down. "What do you mean, proper?"

She lifted one shoulder modestly. "I learned on my own, in a vessel much smaller and older than this one. I should like to learn better skills one day."

"*You* can pilot an airship?"

"Yes. I brought Louise Thorne's vessel back from Venice last week. Alone. After having been fired upon by a steam cannon."

"Good heavens." His shock was tempered with admiration. "There is more to you than meets the eye." Then he seemed to recall the role he had meant to play. "Mind you, what meets the eye is very pleasing indeed."

"Thank you, Your Grace. I am sure that our hosts will be looking for us. Shall we join them?"

"In a moment." He touched her hand. "Please tell me that you will be attending the Maifest Ball."

"I had planned to accompany Lady Thorne, yes."

He stood very close. Much too close for comfort, but she had made up her mind to pursue this course, so she couldn't very well back away now.

"They always make me open balls with the daughter of the house," he confided, "but Maifest is different. It is held at Nymphenburg, in the great double courtyard, and everyone is invited. Will you partner me for the first dance?"

Her lashes fluttered up, then down. "Waltz or polka?"

"Even if it was a polka, I'd make them play a waltz so that I might hold you."

No doubt he would. "I would be honored, Your Grace. And now I hear the count's voice. You must join him or risk scandal."

"I love a good scandal." He grinned, his teeth white in the brush of his beard and moustache, but at least he took her at her word, and stepped lightly up the steps to meet Count von Zeppelin in the corridor.

Georgia took a deep breath, gazing out the viewing ports at the huge crowd gathered in the hangar, clearly waiting for their turn to view the new ship. So she would open the ball with him. And very likely go in to supper together. And have an invitation to the hunting lodge by the end of the evening.

Now all she had to do was manage him with a firm hand, and she might come out of this with more than her reputation still intact.

Nymphenburg, at noon

L—, G—,

I have a tiny puzzle to show you when we meet. I am to attend the automaton empress to the Museum of Natural History this afternoon to open a new wing. Upon our return at three, I will invite it to my rooms for tea, where I hope to find you paying a call. This will be your opportunity, Louise, to get its back up and see what it will tell us.

I confess I am anxious to know. The atmosphere here is very strange. Everyone behaves as though the empress is a human and the only oddity is her ladies all being away. Of course they must be away, for the jig would be up in minutes if people who actually knew her were to see her close to. I do not know how the staff do not see it. Then again, they seem to keep their eyes down and their heads low.

I predict my own unmasking will come sooner rather than later, but hopefully not before we have completed our inquiries. Meanwhile, please do not forget to bring the jewels when you come.

M.

The tube whooshed away toward Kastanienhof, unbeknownst to anyone, for Millie was alone. Even Lisabet had gone for her midday meal. The moment the silver luncheon tray was brought to her room by a footman in livery, Millie understood that the automaton was not to dine with her, nor was she to be escorted upstairs to dine in lonely state in the empress's private dining room, as her ladies normally would.

It was a relief, really. The less Millie was seen about the royal apartments, the less her chances of running into someone who actually knew the Margravine von Karlsrühe. Whoever was dressing the automaton might be able to keep food and drink away from it for some little time longer, though how this farce was to go on with the Maifest Ball and all its food approaching, she did not know. In any case, her own luncheon was very good—broiled trout in herbs with lemon, and more of the divine white asparagus of which she was becoming very fond.

The schedule instructed her to present herself in the empress's rooms at ten minutes past one, and when she did so, she found the automaton dressed to go out. Who had dressed it? That was the question she must answer—today, if possible. Outside of asking the automaton point blank and giving her own game away, she was determined to find out what mysterious, invisible persons were making the machine do their bidding.

Once she knew that, then perhaps she might have a clue as to the whereabouts of the real empress.

When she rose from her curtsey, the automaton said calmly, "If you are ready, Margravine, I am informed the landau is waiting." It glided away, its steps smooth and unfaltering under the apricot skirts of its afternoon gown and a knee-length fine wool coat so beautifully cut and trimmed that Georgia would have sighed in delight.

But Georgia and her skill at conversation were not here, so it was up to Millie to make small talk with the automaton all the way across town. Fortunately, the machine treated remarks about the weather with the same calm gravity as it had the news of the Doge's perfidy in Venice—as though both subjects weighed the same. Which, Millie supposed, they did. The automaton took in information and spat it back out upon request, with no room in the middle for either opinion or emotion.

A shiver crept up her back, and she shifted on the landau's velvet seat. Luckily, its liveried pilot and the escorts ahead of and behind them paid no attention to her at all.

They were met at the foot of the marble steps by a delegation consisting of the directors of the museum and the mayor of Munich. Other than politely removing their hats in acknowledgment of Millie's position at court and murmuring politenesses, no one spoke to her as she followed the automaton up the steps and across the vast foyer crowded with cheering people to the entrance to the new wing.

The automaton waved gracefully to the crowd. The managing director politely indicated that it should cut a red ribbon stretched across the grand double doors with a pair of silver scissors. It carried out this task with aplomb, and as the ribbons fluttered to the floor, the crowd applauded. An escorted tour of the displays in the new wing followed, which consist mostly of enormous rocks with the skeletons of primeval creatures imprisoned in them. Teddy would have been most intrigued. Perhaps someday they could return to Munich and she could show him, while regaling him with the tale of her impersonating a lady in waiting every bit as much as the automaton was impersonating its maker.

The automaton remained polite and interested, and in fact seemed to synthesize some of the information it was receiving, collate it with what it may have heard read from a newspaper, and ask what appeared to be intelligent questions. At any moment, Millie expected that its impersonation would be discovered, but no one seemed to think its behavior anything out of the ordinary. Was the empress held in such a deep respect that no one would admit how out of character her behavior was?

It was an enormous relief to be handed once more into the landau and be conveyed back across town to the palace. This time Millie did not converse, as a kind of test. The automaton did not seem offended, but neither did it make small talk of its own to fill the silence. It was rather like riding in a very ostentatious vehicle with a teakettle. Or a mother's helper.

When they reached the royal apartments once more, Millie stopped the automaton's progress into the vestibule by the simple expedient of blocking the doorway.

"Your Imperial Majesty, I would like nothing more than some refreshment after such a stimulating afternoon. Would you care to join me in my rooms? Well, they are Baroness Salzmann's rooms, but they are lent to me until she returns."

Belatedly, she wondered what she would do if the thing declined. Was it capable of independent decisions, or would it simply go where it was instructed?

"I am afraid my schedule dictates that I am to rest now," it said pleasantly. "I do need rest after public engagements. They are very wearing, are they not?"

"I could not agree more, Ma'am." *Instructions. Hmm. Well, nothing ventured, nothing gained.* "Please come with me now. I am expecting friends of yours and they would be so disappointed not to see you."

"Friends of mine?"

"Yes—Lady Louise Thorne." *Please let her have received my*

note and be waiting. Otherwise Millie would have no idea what to do with the creature other than send it back to its rooms and hope it didn't repeat her odd behavior to whoever waited there.

"I know Lady Thorne well," it said, as though reminding itself. "I should be pleased to join you. Thank you."

Millie's relief turned to surprise when it became clear almost immediately that the automaton also knew exactly where Baroness Salzmann's rooms were.

She tested it again. "Before we go in, Ma'am, I wonder if you might show me where the Landgräfin Winter's rooms are?"

"Certainly." It pointed down the corridor. "The second door on the left, there. But she is not here. She is at Linderhof, awaiting my arrival."

"Of course, Ma'am, how silly of me. Perhaps, then, you might know where I might find Lady Hilda Meissen's rooms. A—a note came to mine in error." Lady Hilda was one of the newer ladies in waiting, from one of the smaller hereditary principalities, and also conveniently at Linderhof.

"I am not expected to know where all my ladies are accommodated," the automaton said. "You must ask Herr Doktor Mainz for information of that kind."

"Thank you, Ma'am, I shall."

How interesting. The thing knew where Lady Winter's apartments were, and Lady Salzmann's, but not the others? It was understandable that it might know the rooms of Christina's chief attendant, the one of highest rank, who directed the activities of the others. But why the latter, when the young baroness was so new?

But there was no time to wonder. She opened the door of

her suite and waited for the automaton to precede her. And there was Louise Thorne waiting for them, with a pot of tea and a cake stand loaded with delectables, which sat on the low table between the sofas.

"Your Imperial Majesty." Louise dropped into a curtsey while Millie did her best not to faint from sheer relief.

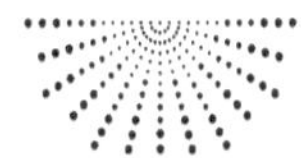

ith some dexterity of mind, Georgia managed to decline all Archduke Rupert's offers to convey her to her next engagement, no matter where it was. In the end she lost him in the refreshment tents, snatched up a sausage wrapped in flaky pastry, and hastened out to the road to board the tram.

She disembarked near Kastanienhof and walked down its cool, chestnut-shaded avenue with a sense of homecoming. The singing sound of a landau puttering up behind made her turn.

"Auntie Georgia!" Cora tumbled out of it and, smiling, the chauffeur continued on his way to the mews behind the house. "Have you been out?"

"I have indeed. I went to the Zeppelin Airship Works to see their new civilian vessel, and who should I meet but Count von Zeppelin, his wife, and Archduke Rupert."

"The new vessel!" the child cried, clearly not impressed by counts or archdukes. "Oh, how I wish I could have gone."

"The ship will be trundling about in the sky for some

years, my dear. Your education is the most important thing now."

Cora made a face and ran on ahead. By the time Georgia reached the door, Cora had come back outside with a note. "Mama is not at home, but she left you this."

3:00 p.m.

Georgia,

I have been summoned to N. by M. She will lure the automaton to her rooms—the rest is up to me. And you, if you arrive in time. Come at once.

In haste—

L.

Georgia handed it to Cora, who read it in the space of a breath. "Auntie Georgia, please don't make me stay home while you do something exciting."

"Certainly not." After repeated kidnapping attempts in Venice, Georgia no longer felt comfortable leaving the child by herself, at home with staff known to her or not. "I hope we can forage for some tea at the palace. My throat is as dry as a desert. Run and tell the chauffeur his duties are not yet concluded for the day."

With a whoop that would have made Marcus Seacombe proud, Cora sped off to the mews, and in a few minutes the Thorne landau puttered up to the front stairs, Cora in the navigator's chair up front. Georgia climbed into the rear compartment, and they were on their way.

At Nymphenburg, the guards at the door recognized her, inclined their heads, and allowed them to enter the massive, echoing foyer. She only had to ask for directions once before she found her way to the suites of the ladies in waiting, and was admitted by a clearly relieved Millie.

"Is it still here?" Cora whispered, taking Millie's hand. "I want to see it."

"You shall not only see it, but I will present you," Millie whispered back. "Remember, for purposes of our inquiries, it is the empress and I am the margravine."

Millie and Louise were halfway through a cup of tea and some cakes, while the automaton pretended to be distracted by the view of the gardens so as to avoid having any. Cora was presented, made a curtsey that was a model of perfection, and upon being raised by the automaton, withdrew. She and Georgia fell upon the comestibles like a pair of hawks.

After a minute or two, Louise drained her cup and leaned toward them. "No time like the present," she whispered. "Georgia, I do hope you feel up to a bit of wrestling if it refuses me."

Cora's eyes widened, speechless since her mouth was full. Georgia swallowed her bit of egg tart rather suddenly, and had to take a gulp of tea. "I shall follow your lead," she whispered back, feeling rather rash. How strong *was* the wretched thing?

Louise walked up to it with every appearance of confidence. "Christina, I must examine your clockwork. You have developed a tic."

"I am the empress," the automaton said. "You must not be so familiar."

"You are Christina, the automaton," Louise said firmly. "Turn your back toward me so that I may unhook your bodice and make an adjustment."

"I am not to be touched."

Had it been instructed to say this should anyone try what Louise was trying? Or was it simply continuing to act its part?

"Christina, obey me at once."

The automaton paused, but Georgia could not tell whether it was struggling with conflicting instructions, or simply trying to remember where it had heard Louise's voice before.

"I know Lady Thorne well." It turned and presented its back to Louise.

Louise closed her eyes briefly and exhaled in relief. "Thank you, Christina."

Swiftly, before the machine changed gears, she unhooked the back of its dress. Georgia put down her tea and hastened over—the opportunity to look at the construction of such a luscious gown was irresistible.

While she examined boning and lining, Louise whipped off the delicate lawn chemise and removed a figure shaper from the automaton's torso, revealing a smooth skinlike back with the outline of a square taking up most of it. Louise pressed on one corner, and it popped open to reveal innards much more complicated even than an automaton intelligence system in an airship. Much smaller, for one thing. The automaton had no spine or ribs, but instead a wilderness of clockwork, brass and steel gears, and tiny filaments that might have been miniature pulleys or, for all Georgia knew, its nervous system. Lights flickered here and there within the strands, but what their purpose was, she dared not ask.

Frowning with concentration, Louise did something inside the cavity that looked like someone playing a very tiny piano, and the automaton began to speak.

I know Lady Thorne well.
I am not to be touched.
You must not be so familiar. I am the empress.
How do you do, Miss Thorne.
What a lovely view you have here, Margravine.

THE HAIRS ROSE on Georgia's scalp as she realized the automaton was reciting the last ten minutes of its own speech in reverse.

"I am afraid we must go back through at least four days' worth of memory," Louise said rather apologetically. "When we get to Sunday, I will expand its recall to the voices of others. They will still be backwards, but hopefully we will get the gist of it."

"I shall write it down," Cora said.

"Stationery is in the desk," Millie told her. "I hope you write quickly."

"I know shorthand," the ten-year-old informed her proudly, and took up her station at the delicate little desk. "I taught myself from a code book last Christmas holidays."

Of course she had.

"Oh dear, this is today, at the museum," Millie said, listening. "In a moment you will hear her talking about the weather with me." After a moment, she leaned forward, her tea forgotten. "Ask her to repeat everything now. I want to know if her dresser converses with her."

Louise made an adjustment, and to Georgia's astonishment, another person's voice could be heard, speaking in German.

Very good, Your Imperial Majesty.

I am the empress. I am not to be touched.

You will do. Off you go. What do you say when
people get too close?

This dress is wasted on you, but I suppose we
must keep up appearances.

Now the wig.

Christina, stand still. You need a figure shaper,
remember? Oh, why am I talking to it.

CORA'S POTHOOKS marched across a page of stationery. Louise made another adjustment and other speakers were omitted while the automaton resumed repeating itself. Here was her speech to the graduating students of the Lycée. And a meeting of some civic delegation from Österreich.

Georgia returned to Millie, took a tea cake, and whispered, "Did you recognize the dresser's voice?"

"No." Millie frowned. "But I will remember it. The person is a woman, of course, but German is not her mother tongue. Did you hear? She does not pronounce certain sounds properly—sounds with the umlaut. I cannot help but notice should I hear that again."

What a good thing Millie's ear for languages was more finely tuned than Georgia's! It had certainly served them well since they had departed England's green and pleasant land.

An hour passed with excruciating slowness as the automaton regurgitated what it had said and occasionally, what it had heard. It was taking so long to revisit the days that Georgia began to wonder when the alarm would be raised at its absence.

"What engagements is it missing?" she whispered to Millie. "We shall be discovered."

Millie took a leather folder identical to that of Landgräfin Winter from the table and perused the empress's schedule. "Nothing until five. It said it was supposed to rest when we came back from the museum. I wonder what it actually does?"

"Perhaps someone does what we are doing," she suggested. "Perhaps they pick up state secrets like breadcrumbs, walking backward."

The chronometer read four-fifteen. Would that give them enough time to reach the day they needed?

You are very welcome to our court today, Lady Langford, Miss Brunel.

Ah. They had arrived at Monday. "Not much longer," she said to Millie.

Another agonizing half hour passed before Louise looked up. "Oh, dear. I think we have it. Cora, be ready."

> *I am the empress. I am not to be touched.*
> You will return to the empress's apartments. You
>   are not to be touched.
> *[A brief silence.]*
> How dare you? What are you—
> *[A sound like a muffled scream.]*
> No, Ma'am. I have this.
> Hello. I understand you have tidings of my lady
>   in waiting?
> Good afternoon, Ma'am.
> *[A man's voice. A pause.]*
> Very well—show them in. They will forgive me
>   if I finish this repair to the automaton's foot.

> She seems to have sustained a little damage. I
> wonder if she kicked something?
> It is, Ma'am.
> Good afternoon, Herr Doktor. It must be very
> urgent for you to interrupt me in the
> laboratory.
> Good afternoon, Ma'am. A messenger has come
> from Baroness Salzmann.

Cora looked up. "Is there more?"

Back in time they went, but there was only a long stretch of silence. "It must have been in the laboratory some time before she had an opportunity to work on it," Louise said. "I think we have gleaned all we can."

Georgia wished she had a shawl to wrap around herself against the memory of that scream.

Swiftly, Louise dressed the machine. "Don't you find it interesting that the automaton repeats certain phrases? I wonder if it is a code, such as the automaton intelligence systems obey. When I say, *Thetis, bear two points to starboard,* my ship obeys me. What if we perform a little experiment?" She fastened the last hook and smoothed the fabric, then went around to adjust the flounces of chiffon on the front. "You are the empress. You are not to be touched."

"I am the empress. I am not to be touched." The automaton turned. "Margravine von Karlsrühe, when is my next engagement?"

Millie fumbled for the leather folder. "You are to attend a reception for the ambassador from the Fifteen Colonies, Ma'am, at seven-thirty, with a private audience to follow."

"Very well. You will attend me, of course."

"Of course," Millie said faintly.

The automaton glided toward the door, and Millie barely got there in time to open it. Both Georgia and Louise were taken aback when Millie closed the door and returned to the sofa.

"Aren't you going to help her change?" Georgia asked. "Won't it be noticed?"

"I do want to go upstairs, but I suspect I will find her unavailable while the mystery woman dresses her," Millie said. "In any case, there might be too many people about her apartments just now. I will make an attempt to surprise this dresser after the reception, when I am with the automaton and it would seem natural for me to stay with her. Oh, please tell me you brought some jewels for me."

Georgia stared, then looked from Millie to Louise. "Jewels?"

"Yes—did you not receive the two tubes I sent?"

"Oh, dear." Louise hurried over and sat upon the sofa facing them. "I never thought to check."

"Nor did I," Georgia admitted. "I am so sorry, Millie."

"I am most sorry of all," Cora said in a small voice. She turned out her pockets and produced two envelopes. "I checked the communications cabinet and then we left in such a hurry, I forgot. Please forgive me, Auntie Millie."

Millie was clearly trying to be brave. "Of course, child."

Georgia and Louise scanned the notes briefly. In Cora's defense, no one had been home to look out the jewelry, and other matters had seemed more pressing at the time. "I did bring a small tiara with me, along with the sapphires. But it is already after four. Is there time for us to drive to Kastanienhof and back?"

"I'm afraid not," Louise said.

Millie had been slumped in dismay, but now she straightened. "Georgia, if I might borrow that necklace you have on, I shall simply fasten it about my head in a fillet and hope no one notices."

"Perhaps you will start a new fashion," Cora said hesitantly, with an air of looking on the bright side. Then she slunk back to the desk and began diligently to copy out the automaton's conversation from her pothooks, as though hoping this would make up for her forgetfulness.

"The lucky thing about one's being a woman of advanced years is that no one looks at one long enough to start anything at all—even a conversation." Millie smiled at them. "I am being quite serious. Age is almost a disguise in itself."

"Your years are hardly advanced, my dear." Georgia removed the Langford pearls, and was astonished to see that, wrapped about Millie's head à la Millais or Mucha, they did rather look like a diadem. "I have a better idea. Let us dispense with your everyday style altogether and French braid them into a crown."

Twenty minutes later, Millie turned this way and that in front of the cheval glass. "Lovely. This will do very well. Thank you."

She did look lovely. Pearls seemed to suit her.

"And it has the advantage of making them impossible to lose or steal," Louise pointed out.

Cora's spirits seemed to have returned. "I've finished what the automaton said—and put it right way round. Even then, it's very puzzling."

The three of them studied the slightly uneven hand that covered both sides of the piece of palace stationery.

"*Herr Doktor* … that must be Herr Doktor Mainz, the master of the household," Millie said. "He met me this morning and showed me to these rooms."

"It's a pity he seems to have left her alone with her caller," Louise said, her gaze on the transcript. "Had he not, Christina might still be with us. Who was her visitor—or should I say, kidnapper? And how did he spirit her out of the palace?"

"He had to have had help." Millie paused. "Possibly even Dr Mainz, though it pains me to say so. He seems very kind."

"You don't recognize the other man's voice, either of you?" Georgia asked.

Louise shook her head.

"I might ask Dr Mainz who it was," Millie said. "But on what pretext? Without the automaton, we would not have known this conversation ever happened. And we were not even in the palace on Sunday. We were at Kastanienhof—and he of all people will know it."

"I don't think you should ask him, Millie," Georgia said thoughtfully. "If this Dr Mainz was involved, questions will alarm him. I could not bear for you to meet the same fate."

"But how was it managed?" Louise demanded of the room in general. "An anointed monarch does not simply sink through the floor. Someone must have seen her leave, whether willingly or no."

"Oh!" Millie jumped up and hurried into the bedroom, returning with her pocketbook. "I cannot blame Cora for forgetting the tubes, when I have forgotten what I told you in the one I sent first. Look. The maid Lisabet confirmed the hand is Baroness Salzmann's."

She moved the teapot and laid the torn pieces in order on the table.

Cora joined them to read the unfinished note. "*Take to your burrow and hide in the dark with the others,*" she read aloud. "What does that mean? For they cannot be badgers, or moles. Are there tunnels under this palace, Mama?"

"If there are, I am not privy to them. And the only hidden staircases I have ever seen are those used by the staff." She paused, staring into space for a moment. "She could not have meant the pump system, surely."

Georgia and Millie waited. Georgia was still wondering about the ominous *others* the baroness had mentioned. How many others? And were they really hiding, or was it a figure of speech? Was there some group with a grudge against the young empress?

"The pumps for the fountains?" Cora's forehead wrinkled. "A person cannot fit inside the pipes, Mama."

"No, but Christina's laboratory is in the wing where the old duke's orangerie was located a century ago. At one end is the Johannis pump. There is underground access to it, so that the duke was not disturbed in his meditations."

"Could that be what she meant by *your burrow?*" Cora suggested, still clearly attempting to puzzle out the baroness's note.

"It is the closest we have at the moment," her mother said thoughtfully. "Millie, you must change—it is nearly five o'clock. Georgia, if you would, go with Lehrer—our driver—and tell him that Cora and I will be with him in twenty minutes at the east gate. Then we shall go home."

"Where are we going, Mama?"

"To the Johannis pump. If we are very lucky, we may find a clue that confirms the empress was forcibly removed."

CHAPTER EIGHT

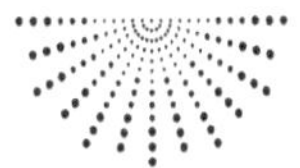

Wednesday, May 15, 1895
5:00 p.m.

Twenty minutes later, the tall wrought-iron gates on the east side of the palace swung open enough to allow Louise and Cora to slip out. They made certain it latched and locked, then climbed into the waiting landau with Georgia.

From the sparkle of pent-up excitement in Cora's eyes, and the snap of indignation in those of Louise, they had found something. But nothing could be revealed until they were back at Kastanienhof, with its thick walls.

When they walked into the vestibule, an astonishing sight met Georgia's eyes. On the sideboard where normally there rested a silver tray with the post and any condolences that had been personally delivered, was a bouquet of at least three dozen red roses, arranged in a crystal vase.

"Good heavens, did someone empty the hothouse?" Louise peered at the small envelope. "Why, Georgia, they're for you."

With a sinking feeling she knew the sender, Georgia unfolded the note, which was written in a flawless formal hand.

My dear Lady Langford,

I cannot stop thinking of you—imagining these soft petals against your skin as you breathe in their fragrance. I hope they will make you think of me, too.

R dux

She made a choked sound and crumpled the note, thrusting it into her pocket.

The scent of the roses followed them upstairs, where Louise pulled Georgia into the small sitting room off her bedroom, and Cora closed the door.

"Were those roses from the archduke?"

"Yes, but never mind him." Georgia removed her hat and wrestled her thoughts into more useful channels. "You found something in the laboratory, didn't you?"

She and Cora settled on the little brocade divan.

"We did indeed." Louise tossed her own hat on a spindly side table, seated herself, and leaned forward so that she might lower her voice. "It is clear that few have been in there since Sunday. Granted, Christina finds the only privacy she is permitted to know in her laboratory, and will not allow the staff to clean it. However, the odd messenger and Dr Mainz do come and go." She glanced at her daughter, as though to invite her to take up the story.

"We found a turnscrew on the floor, and a small drawer had been pulled out of the bench. Some of the little bolts in it spilled on the floor," Cora said. "They had been cleaned up, but there were still a few that had rolled under the bench."

"Signs of a struggle?" Georgia hazarded.

"It appears that way," Louise replied. "The empress can be disorderly in some aspects of her daily life, but never in her schedule or her laboratory. She can lay hands on anything from a speaking horn to the smallest gear that makes the automaton blink within seconds. She would never leave parts or tools on the floor to be stepped on."

"So while one or more someones did the abducting, another stayed behind to tidy up," Georgia mused, seeing the scene in her mind's eye. "And the tunnel?"

"Here is where it becomes interesting. Do you remember we spoke of breadcrumbs earlier?"

Cora opened her palm, revealing two tiny objects.

"The aforementioned bolts?" Georgia peered at them.

"One just inside the door to the access tunnel, dropped close to the wall so it wouldn't be noticed by the chap following. Another outside on the ground, where we found wheel marks in the dirt."

"The wheels of what sort of vehicle?"

"Someone was familiar with that tunnel, and has a key to the outer door, which narrows the possibilities to engineers and groundskeepers," Louise said. "My money is on the former. There are vehicles the groundskeepers use to get about, however—you've seen how enormous the park is. Bundle her into a steam lorry full of tree trimmings and no one would think anything of it."

"Even in broad daylight," Cora put in. She put the two tiny bolts back in her pocket. "We searched the ground in widening circles, and found one near the gate where you met us."

"So they removed her forcibly and presumably prevented her from calling out in some way. But she was conscious—still able to think and act," Georgia said. "Brave young woman. The question now is, how are we to find out where she has been taken?"

"I hope she is being held somewhere," Louise said unhappily. "The other two options are grim indeed."

Georgia could imagine only one grim option. "What is the second?"

Louise rose and walked to the window, where she gazed out at the lake. "That she staged her own kidnapping, and has voluntarily walked out of her own life. Has abdicated the throne."

"Why on earth would she do that?" Georgia felt a little winded. This possibility had never once occurred to her.

"She is an engineering genius," Louise said to the window. "It is the calling she loves, not the crown. If a woman may marry for love and give up her freedom, may she not walk away from a palace for love, and restore it?"

"She may well do so, but what then? A woman brought up to occupy a throne may not simply put on an overall and take up a wrench as an apprentice in some steamworks."

"Empress Christina could," Cora said with certainty.

"But a woman with her skills would be more likely to distinguish herself—present monographs at international conferences—establish her own works as Count von Zeppelin did," Georgia argued. "Even teach applied engineering at university."

"She could," Louise allowed. "But until those lofty goals are reached, she must feed, clothe, and house herself. That humble steamworks would allow the more everyday requirements to be met—and provide excellent cover besides."

Dissatisfied, Georgia took an agitated turn about the room. It was only ten steps across, so it did not take long to circumnavigate it. "I cannot think it of her. And in your heart, you do not, either, Louise."

"No, I do not. For what I have left out of my homely little picture is her sense of duty. Her attention to her schedule is only the smallest symptom of it. She could have abdicated the crown to Rupert in some private ceremony, but she never will. She would die first."

Cora's lip wobbled. "Do not say that, Mama."

"I speak in a theoretical sense," she assured her daughter, running a hand over her hair, almost as though she were reassuring herself the child was safe. "So of all our options, we have enough evidence to make kidnapping the most reasonable. Not staged, but real. The question is, what now?"

"We must find out from this Dr Mainz whom he admitted to the laboratory that day," Georgia said. It seemed their only clue. "But how are we to do that without revealing that the empress is missing?"

"Millie could ask him," Cora suggested.

"I hesitate to bring suspicion upon Millie by having her make too many inquiries," Georgia said. "She is our most valuable source of information at the moment, and I do not want to put her in jeopardy."

"She is alone, and vulnerable," Louise said by way of agreement. "We must think of something else."

Silence fell, broken only by a sparrow landing on the window ledge to peer in at them.

"What about that maid?" Georgia said suddenly. "Lisabet, who works in the baroness's suite of rooms."

"The more we widen our circle beyond we four, the more difficult it will be to keep our inquiries secret," Louise warned.

"We do not have to mention our inquiries. What if Millie were to ask Lisabet to ask Dr Mainz who the person was. Say the empress wishes to write a note and could not remember the name."

"Then it would be easier for Millie to ask him herself, and we are back to square one," Louise said.

Georgia frowned. If not Lisabet, they had no other options. "Perhaps Cora is right, and Millie is our best choice," she said at last. "The fewer we bring into our circle, the safer we are—and the safer the empress might be. I will send a note to ask her if she feels up to taking this risk."

Dearest,

Proof of forced removal has been found. It is imperative we know who was the third party in the laboratory. Could you ask the good Doktor for a name on some pretext—perhaps the empress wishes to send the man a note? However, if you do not wish to do so, we understand and will find another way.

Meanwhile, I must prepare for Maifest. The most vulgar bouquet of red roses was waiting for me just now, with a nauseating note. I do hope the royal sender is not about to present himself likewise. I shall be quite put off my feed.

G.

6:45 p.m.

Lisabet had returned with Millie's dinner on a tray, and

afterward, had stayed to help her dress for the ambassador's reception that evening. As she was buttoned and hooked into her evening gown of rose silk trimmed in velvet and lace, Millie became more determined to attend the automaton to her rooms following the reception, and stay either until she found out who its dresser was, or was commanded to leave. If she failed on that head, then she might still succeed with Georgia's commission to ask Dr Mainz about the empress's visitor.

Granted, it was only her first day in the palace, and they had seen success with the automaton's memory. Though *success* was a relative term, if it had led to proof that the real empress had indeed been abducted. What they were going to do about a crime so serious was a mystery. She could only hope she would be as successful in winkling the information about the miscreant's identity out of Dr Mainz.

But first things first.

"Thank you, Lisabet. While I do not quite feel equal to my first reception, luckily this dress is equal to anything."

"Of course you will be, Margravine. And may I say that this new way of doing your hair is lovely. If only the other ladies were here to see!"

She really was a dear. Millie smiled with some affection and rustled away, climbing the staircases to the empress's rooms while chanting *chin up, chin up* in her head.

Since this was a formal occasion, she and the empress were preceded into the audience chamber by the Minister of Foreign Affairs and two footmen, which relieved her of the need for any conversation. The reception itself demanded not much from the royal lady except to stand upon the bottom step of the dais with Millie behind her, smile, and receive the bows and greetings of the ambassador from the Fifteen Colonies, one Archibald Silverton.

Then he turned to beckon forward someone in the crowd, and Millie's heart nearly stopped in her chest.

"Your Imperial Majesty, I believe you are acquainted with Mr Cornelius van Meere, the renowned engineering genius, businessman, and railroad baron from the Texican Territory?"

Mr van Meere bowed low and when he straightened, his gaze fell like a thunderbolt on Millie, who was standing at the automaton's left shoulder, stricken speechless.

He turned scarlet, then realized that the automaton was speaking to him, welcoming him back to the Kingdom of Prussia. He blinked. Stared fixedly at the royal personage to whom he had just been presented. Turned pale.

And Millie knew at once he had recognized the automaton.

Hadn't Louise told them he had visited the empress's laboratory? For all Millie knew, some of the parts inside it had been brought from his manufactories in his own pockets.

Oh my goodness, sir, please keep silent. Please don't give the game away.

"May I present my lady in waiting, the Margravine von Karlsrühe, from the north of our empire?" the automaton said.

Millie curtsied to the ambassador and Mr van Meere, grateful as never before for the rigid demands of precedence, which dictated that as a lady of rank, she should be introduced first. Now Mr van Meere would know she was incognito, and would not address her with the familiarity of a man who had fished her out of a lagoon and tossed her soaking wet into a fishing boat less than a week ago.

"And this is my friend and traveling companion, Mr Dustin Seacombe," Mr van Meere said in return.

Goodness gracious. Mr Seacombe's considering gaze met Millie's seconds before he swept off his disreputable Stetson and bowed low to the automaton, who welcomed him cordially.

What on earth were they doing here? They were supposed to be across the Atlantic by now, not standing about in tie and tails (well, Mr van Meere was, at least) in a city they had departed three days ago!

What will Georgia say? I must send a tube as soon as I can.

There was no opportunity to speak further, for others from the ambassador's delegation must be introduced, and the two Texicans faded back into the crowd … as much as two tall, tanned men were able to. From the corner of her eye Millie kept track of their movements until at last the formalities were completed and the automaton descended from the dais.

It spent exactly a quarter of an hour exchanging pleasantries with the ambassador, while the Minister of Foreign Affairs hinted at a longer meeting in more businesslike surroundings. Then the automaton turned to Millie.

"Margravine, I shall meet privately with our guest, and then retire. I believe there are to be refreshments and possibly dancing. You are welcome to stay if it pleases you."

Millie felt as though she were being pulled in two equally urgent directions. How could she stay—and miss the opportunity to find out who was dressing the automaton? Yet, how could she leave without speaking to Mr van Meere and learning why they were here?

After a struggle, duty and their inquiries won. "Ma'am, indeed not. I will wait, and then attend you to your rooms."

"No, no. I insist. You must represent me to this company."

"The Minister of Foreign Affairs is doing that most admirably. Come, Ma'am, after your meeting I will see you to your private apartments."

"I wish you to stay."

It gazed at her and did not blink.

Millie's courage failed her at the thought that the automaton remembered its conversations. If she insisted on her own way, and if, as they suspected, someone listened to its memories during the day, that person might become suspicious.

"Of course, Ma'am. Please send for me if you need me."

"Certainly. Good evening."

Millie curtsied to the floor until the automaton was the requisite three paces away, then rose. The ambassador followed it, two footmen bringing up the rear as it made its graceful way through the doors and out of sight.

Very well. She would simply follow it upstairs as soon as she could, and take an inventory of persons in the private apartments. That list of possibilities was a beginning, at least.

"May I take the liberty of saying, Margravine, that you look particularly lovely this evening."

The rumble of that voice seemed to create ripples in her very blood. When she turned, Millie found the two Texicans standing close by, but only one of them had been watching the automaton leave the audience chamber.

Mr van Meere was looking down at her with unmitigated delight. "Please tell me there's a good yarn behind this unexpected meeting."

"Indeed there is, but I cannot tell it just now. What on earth are you doing here, sir? I thought you were on the other side of the Atlantic."

"So we were—halfway, at least. Until we received a pigeon. An urgent *m'aidez* to anyone within half a day's flight of the ambassador's private airship, which had been attacked by air pirates and had gone down west of the Azores. We made pretty fast time back to it, and while it was too late to save the cargo, at least we could collect Silverton and the crew and some odds and ends they were bringing over. Then we took them to The Hague to report the crime. We landed here this afternoon, with just enough time for Silverton to borrow some finer feathers than he had on, and here we are."

"You carry fine feathers with you on your voyages?" She tried not to look him up and down, but she was very much aware of the manly figure he cut, with those broad, capable shoulders and mechanic's strong hands.

"They come in useful, as I'm sure you've discovered, Margravine," Mr Seacombe said smoothly. "May I ask if your family are all well?"

"They are indeed, sir," she said pleasantly. "One or two are visiting friends here. I saw them only this afternoon, in fact. I would invite you to dinner, or even tea, but as you see, my duties to Her Imperial Majesty keep me here at Nymphenburg. You see, I am to attend the empress until the return of Baroness Salzmann, who has gone home due to—" She looked around as though to spot someone they might know, but no one was within earshot. She lowered her voice. "A sudden and unexpected weight gain."

Mr van Meere looked blank. Mr Seacombe, the only one who was a father, drew in a breath. "I see."

"Yes, it was most surprising, considering she had only been here four months. But I welcomed the chance to take her place in the empress's service."

"That must have taken some doing," Mr Seacombe murmured.

"We must catch up on our news," Mr van Meere said. "Particularly in light of the empress's, er, state of health. May we fix a time and place?"

"I am afraid my time is at her disposal," Millie said with real regret, "but I am anxious for a visit. She tends to rest between the hours of three and five—"

"Rest?" Mr van Meere blurted, clearly in disbelief.

For of course automatons did not rest. Nor did the empress, but that was neither here nor there. "Yes. Which means I am free to make my own engagements during that time. If you could convey me to their house, I am sure my friends would welcome you."

"Done," he said. "Seacombe?"

"Of course," he growled, as if this were so obvious it did not need confirmation. "Is Marcus also welcome?"

"I should be vexed if he were not," Millie said. "So would another young lady of my acquaintance."

"We will be waiting at the front steps at three, then," Mr van Meere said.

The orchestra began to wheeze and tootle, tuning up for the dancing. "Do you plan to dance?"

"Only if you will oblige me."

Oh, if only it were any other night but this—in any other place but this! "I am afraid I really must return to my duties. I am in pursuit of the solution, you see." She tried to layer as much meaning as she could into the words.

Mr van Meere might move slowly in body, but his brain had the speed and power of a lightning bolt. "So is such a substitution the accepted custom in these parts?"

"Indeed not, sir. No one appears to think anything is out of order but me and one or two others, so affairs at court proceed smoothly. I am expecting a—how would you put it? A bit of a dust-up imminently."

"And you are … comfortable in your accommodations?" Mr Seacombe asked.

Comfortable as in *safe*, she translated. "For now. I really must go." She held out a hand, and Mr van Meere bowed, touching his lips to the back of it.

A tingle traveled up Millie's arm and she pulled her hand away before she did something ridiculous, like break out in goosebumps.

"Good evening, then," she said, and hurried away, back straight, with all the dignity that befit a lady of rank.

And all the while she felt the weight of two pairs of eyes, filled with justifiable concern, between her shoulders.

The guards stationed on either side of the doors into the royal apartments obligingly opened them, waited for her to rustle through, and closed them behind her. Millie made her approach as quietly as she could, thankful for the thick carpets that disguised the *clack* of her leather-soled shoes. Through the private dining room, the music room where presumably some of the ladies like the Landgräfin Winter played and sang, and the drawing room, until she arrived at last in the corridor housing the closets and their attendant jewelry rooms. Beyond these was the suite overlooking the lake and fountains where the empress slept.

Millie actually had no idea whether the automaton would carry out the impersonation to the point of sleeping in the royal bed, or whether its dresser simply stood it up in a wardrobe until it was time to play its part again.

The closets were her goal now. She was fairly certain she had not been in conversation with Mr van Meere and Mr Seacombe long enough for the audience with the ambassador to have concluded. With any luck, she would be the first to arrive.

The room containing traveling ensembles and day dresses was empty, but it would be, wouldn't it? Millie passed the closet containing tea and dinner gowns and swept into the one for ballgowns and dresses suitable for affairs of state. She came to a confused halt. There were two people in here, neither of whom was the automaton.

They were dressed in the grey gowns and plain white aprons of the empress's personal staff, the same uniform Lisabet wore. At her appearance, they laid down the gown the automaton had been wearing not ten minutes ago, and dipped curtsies.

One began to tuck the gown into its silk dress bag. The other, an older woman, folded her hands before her. "May I be of assistance, Margravine von Karlsrühe?"

"Yes," Millie said, thinking fast. "I have a message for Her Imperial Majesty. I will wait here until her duties are concluded."

"If it pleases you, ma'am, I can convey the message."

Millie frowned. "No, indeed. It is in connection with the

ambassador from the Fifteen Colonies, and was entrusted to me. I shall wait for her. Thank you."

She inclined her head and had half turned to walk the short distance down the corridor to the bedroom door, when the older one said, "Ma'am, the empress has retired and does not wish to be disturbed."

"Retired? Has she already returned?"

"Yes, ma'am."

Impossible. Had the ambassador's meeting been so brief? "She cannot be in bed already. I will not inconvenience her for longer than a minute."

"Ma'am, I beg you will not." Was the maid breathing more quickly? "We have strict instructions that she is not to be disturbed."

"By the staff, perhaps. But not by her own ladies in waiting, who are familiar with her routines and the demands of her position."

The maid gazed at her. Older, early forties perhaps, with blond hair and grey eyes that reminded Millie of the steel ball bearings Teddy had used for marbles as a child. "I understand you are only called to her service today and are not, as you say, familiar with her routines."

"Perhaps not, but I am thoroughly familiar with the expectations of a lady in waiting." She put enough frost in her tone that the younger maid blanched, and fumbled the buttons on the silk bag. "Please do not detain me any longer."

The older one folded her lips together, and Millie hurried down the corridor with a sense of triumph. Georgia would have been proud of her display of backbone—even if it was only acting.

The chased door handle would not turn.

She knocked softly, and hearing no reply, knocked more firmly. "Your Imperial Majesty, it is the Margravine von Karlsrühe. I have a message for you from the delegation."

Silence.

"Ma'am? Is it convenient for you to speak with me?" The automaton should have heard her. Overlooking the utter strangeness of a royal person having no one to wait upon her in a locked bedchamber, at least the automaton was usually polite enough to respond when it was spoken to.

"I told you, Margravine, *Ihre kaiserliche Majestät hat sich zurückgezogen und möchte nicht gestört werden.*"

Millie drew a slow breath. Here were the mispronounced umlauts, just as she had heard them in the automaton's memories. She had found its dresser. No wonder the door was locked. Heaven forbid someone should enter bearing an urgent message and walk in on the automaton—which was probably either completely disrobed or shut up in a wardrobe in truth.

"What is your name?" she inquired, turning.

"Johanna, ma'am. And my companion is Greta."

"Your family name?" Of course she would give an alias.

But the woman did not hesitate. "Fassmacher, ma'am."

"I will abide by the empress's wishes, then, Frau Fassmacher. If you will kindly inform her that I shall attend her after breakfast, I will give her the message then." She paused, and unbent her spine a little. "You do well to defend our mistress's privacy. I wish I had staff half so conscientious."

The woman's body seemed to relax, too, as though mirroring Millie's posture. "Thank you, ma'am. I will tell her you wish to speak to her."

There was nothing further Millie could do except smile

and walk away. And with every step, she put in order what she would tell Georgia. Safely back in her suite of rooms, she sat at the little table and pulled out a sheet of stationery.

G—

Foresight *has returned to Munich with the ambassador to the Fifteen Colonies, having performed a rescue at sea. Its three passengers with whom we are most concerned wish to convey me to Kastanienhof at three o'clock tomorrow so that we may join you for tea.*

I have discovered the dresser's identity after having been refused admittance to the royal bedchamber. I suppose I should have expected to be kept out. I will see what L. knows of her, now that I have a name.

The pearls were a success. No one questioned them. I will return them soonest.

M.

CHAPTER NINE

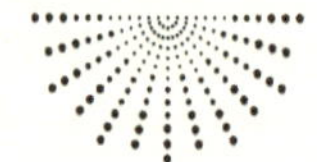

KASTANIENHOF

Thursday, May 16, 1895
3:20 p.m.

Georgia felt as though her heart would beat right out of her chest as Mr van Meere's four-piston landau pulled up in the sweep before the front door. Before it had even come to a halt, Marcus threw up the wing and leaped out of it, to barrel up to Cora with a whoop and a boisterous embrace.

If only the meetings of adults were so artless and easy!

"Marcus," Dustin Seacombe said in his gravelly voice that set her nerves to thrumming, "pay your respects."

Grinning, the boy bobbed a bow that took in all three waiting on the steps. "Lady Thorne, Lady Langford, Miss Brunel. I bet you weren't expecting to see us again so soon."

"The unexpected is rarely such a pleasure," Louise said with a laugh. "Go on, now. We will save you a treat or two from the cake stand—if we are feeling generous."

"It's all right," Cora confided as they ran toward the lake. "I know where there is more."

Throwing the rules of precedence out the window, Cornelius van Meere kissed Millie's hand and made her blush, then bowed to Louise and Georgia. Mr Seacombe contented himself with a bow that, like his son's, took in all three of them. When he straightened and his gaze settled on Georgia, she looked away and turned for the door, following Louise into the house.

A man who had not said good-bye or communicated a single word, though he had the opportunity, was not about to have her attention just because he wanted it.

As they walked into the drawing room with its view of the lake and the children, Mr van Meere was already regaling his hostess with the tale of the daring sea rescue of the ambassador and his party. From her brief but memorable acquaintance with Mr van Meere, Georgia had learned that he was not prone to exaggeration.

"The dam—dashed pirates just left them in the sea to drown, Louise, if you can believe it. Tied up the crew, looted the hold, and flew away without a backward look. I don't think they knew who they had in their hands for ransom. Silverton and his crew got themselves loose, of course, and were able to send a pigeon. The fool pirates never thought to take them with them or destroy them."

"And you have reported the crime, you said," Millie said. "Is there any hope of their being caught?"

"Not my business, if there is," he replied. "But Silverton gave them all the information he could. I hope they are caught, and punished by being dropped out of a hatch, like your Royal Aeronautic Corps used to do in the old days." He took a steaming cup of tea from Louise. "But all that is small potatoes compared to what you ladies have got yourselves mixed up in. What's happened to our friend the empress?"

"If we knew, we should be much closer to finding her," Louise said grimly.

Among the three of them, they brought the two gentlemen up to date, piecing the picture together around the missing figure at the center.

Mr van Meere put down his cup and saucer on his knee rather carefully, as though he thought he might drop them. "And all this has happened since we lifted on Sunday?"

"We believe the abduction occurred Sunday afternoon, while Christina was working in her laboratory. We listened to the automaton's memories yesterday afternoon—"

"Which we believe someone does daily, during the two hours when the royal schedule says she is resting," Millie put in.

"So that's the reason for something everyone knows Christina never does," Mr van Meere said.

"Exactly," Louise said. "I don't think she's had a nap since she was three. In any case, during its memory of that day, a man was admitted to the laboratory whose voice I did not recognize. There was the sound of a scuffle, and Christina protested. Then a prolonged silence until Monday, when it appears the automaton's impersonation began with being prepared for her audience with Georgia and I. We were to brief her on what happened in Venice."

"You realized it was the automaton straight off, of course," Mr Seacombe said. It was the first time he had spoken.

"Of course," Louise replied. "Millie tells me you did, too, Cornelius."

"I never had such a shock in my life. It's had quite a lot done to it since I saw it last."

"But what we do not understand is why no one else seems to know it is the automaton," Georgia said. "It makes me wonder if these new theories of mass delusion might be true."

"Imagine if they *weren't* under a delusion," said Mr Seacombe, his brevity creating its own emphasis.

"That is the difficulty," Louise said. "If it were known that it is not Christina—that she is missing—there would be a constitutional crisis. That idiot Rupert would assume a patched-together regency, and goodness knows what would happen to the Empire."

"Public drunkenness would be made legal, and the harvest festival at Theresienwiese would go on all year round," Georgia said flippantly.

"You know the archduke?" Mr Seacombe said, sounding amused.

"He is responsible for those roses in the vestibule," she said, nettled. "Apparently I am to open the Maifest Ball as his partner."

"What?" Louise's teacup clinked into its saucer, followed by Millie's like a tiny echo.

Georgia nodded, uncertain whether they expected her to feel this was an honor or an unwelcome overture. "He asked me when I joined Count von Zeppelin's party yesterday at the airship works."

"You must have made quite an impression," Millie said faintly.

"Yes, well, that was the plan, wasn't it? I was to be introduced, gain admittance to the royal lodge, and search the place in case there were signs that the empress had been concealed there."

At least she had silenced Mr Seacombe. But not, she was sure, for long. Though the widening of his eyes at these revelations had been most satisfying.

"So you three are investigating her disappearance?" Mr van Meere said with blunt incredulity. "Not the police, or the prime minister, or—or some other man with the authority to locate missing heads of state?"

"You did hear the part about the constitutional crisis, did you not, Cornelius?" Louise said coolly.

"Well, yes, but—"

"Seems a dangerous business," Mr Seacombe said. "Not that the three of you haven't just dealt with a dangerous business recently, and survived."

"With my experience of kidnapping and imprisonment, Louise's in disguise and infiltration, and Millie's in planning escapes, I think we are well qualified to pursue these inquiries, since no one else will," Georgia informed Mr van Meere with some heat. "If anyone in an official capacity were to make the attempt and the word got out, the government would collapse within the week."

"And there are governments who would dearly love to annex unguarded lands," Louise put in. "Those Hapsburgs in particular. To say nothing of the French, to whom two hundred years is nothing. They have not forgotten Napoleon's attempt to conquer Europe, and the price they paid in ceding their territory to the allied powers of the time."

Mr van Meere and his bodyguard exchanged a glance that Georgia could translate word for word. *We can't leave them to manage this alone.*

"There is no need to change your plans—" she began.

"What can we do to help?" Mr Seacombe asked simultaneously.

"I don't know that there is anything you can do," Louise admitted. "I told you of finding the bolts in the tunnel, which prove that she was conscious and able to do what she could to leave a clue. But after she was driven away in some sort of vehicle, the trail goes cold."

"Oh!" Millie sat up straight. "I have not yet told you what I learned last night and this morning. Let me enlighten you all at once."

Both men leaned forward. Louise refilled their cups and passed the cake plate. Mr van Meere took two pieces of fruit-cake rather absently, his gaze not leaving Millie for a moment.

"Last night, after I left our two friends at the reception, I went to the empress's private apartments. I found two maids in the closets, putting away the gown she had worn. When I told them I had a message for the empress, I was told she was not to be disturbed. Which is nonsense. I am her lady in waiting, and it is for the Margravine von Karlsrühe to say who disturbs her royal lady, not a maid."

"Well said." Mr van Meere gulped his tea.

"The door was locked, however, and when no one replied, I imagined the automaton put up in a wardrobe for the night." Mr Seacombe smiled into his cup at the image. "But when the elder of the maids spoke again, I recognized her pronunciation from one of the automaton's memories. Her name is Johanna Fassmacher, and it is she who has been dressing it. I suspect that she or someone giving her orders also arranged the bait and switch with the other ladies in waiting, sending them to Linderhof believing the empress was there." To the gentlemen, she said, "We flew to Linderhof and made the acquaintance of the Landgräfin Winter, who is Mistress of the Robes, and drew her into our confidence. She arranged for me to impersonate the Margravine."

"I did wonder how you pulled that off," Mr van Meere said with admiration.

"Millie, you should expect the ladies to return at any hour," Louise said. "Even with the countess's covering for us, they will not wait much longer for their mistress to turn up at Linderhof."

"What did you learn this morning?" Georgia asked Millie. "For it is too much to hope that you ferreted out the name of the empress's abductor as well."

"One cannot be certain that anyone's names are the real ones, of course," Millie replied, looking rather pleased. "But I did meet Herr Doktor Mainz on the way upstairs to attend the automaton, and asked him for the name of her visitor on Sunday."

"That was bold," Mr Seacombe said in surprise. "Did he tell you?"

"I said that Christina wished to send the man a note, and would he write down the name and the address if he had it."

"In the automaton's memory, it sounded as though the empress was acquainted with him, because she did not hesitate to admit him to her laboratory," Louise said. "Did Dr Mainz cooperate?"

"Yes, with both name and address," Millie said triumphantly, producing a piece of notepaper with four handwritten lines on it. "His name is Fritz Bauer—"

"Bauer!" Mr van Meere repeated.

"—and he has offices here in Munich, in Kaufingerstrasse.

Do you know him?" Millie asked, and with reason, for he had shown too much surprise for it to be a stranger.

"I can't say I know him well," Mr van Meere said. "But I've had some dealings with him. He's a bit of a tinkerer, and a member of that outfit—" He turned to Mr Seacombe. "You know—the one with the twenty-five-cent name."

"The Technical Philosophical Society?"

"That's the one. No idea what it means."

A bell rang in Georgia's memory. "It does mean something —I just read it." She looked around the tidy drawing room. "Louise, what happened to those newspapers I was reading yesterday?"

"I expect they have gone to the kitchen, to light the stove with."

"I will be back in a moment."

She hurried down the stairs to the kitchen, where a question or two located the newspapers, and in particular, *The Scientific Review,* waiting its turn in a box next to the coal scuttle.

On her return to the drawing room, she folded it up to show them the pertinent article. "The archduke went to the Society to bestow some kind of award on Monday, but it seems the engineers weren't as welcoming as he expected. And look." She pointed. "Your Mr Bauer was there as well."

"Secretary of the society, is he?" Mr van Meere mused. He glanced at his companion. "That's a place to start, Seacombe, if you're thinking along the same lines I am."

"Now, see here—" Georgia began. How dared they horn in on an investigation that was proceeding perfectly well, thank you, without their help!

"There is no way round it, Georgia," Louise said with some reluctance.

"Why?" she demanded. "We have agreed that this merits the utmost secrecy and discretion, and we women so far have been able to move about both palace and grounds without drawing attention to ourselves. Why should men become a part of it simply because they have arrived in town and decided they should?"

Louise sighed and her mouth twisted wryly. "Even if one of us went to their offices—even if we were disguised—we should not be allowed past the door. The Technical Philosophical Society admits men only."

"Oh." Georgia deflated, feeling rather foolish.

"Not sure how we're going to weasel the truth out of the man once we see him, mind you," Mr Seacombe went on as if he hadn't heard her outburst. "He's not about to admit he abducted an empress."

"Perhaps you shouldn't approach him at all," Millie suggested, "since Mr van Meere knows him. But it might be useful to follow his movements, in case he knows where she is."

"A sensible man would stay well away," Mr Seacombe said.

"A sensible man wouldn't kidnap a reigning monarch," Millie shot back.

Mr Seacombe smiled, as though she had proved his point. "Luckily for me, I've never met the man. So I might take in a meeting of the Society while Cornelius follows Bauer's trail."

Mr van Meere nodded. "A sound plan. When do we begin?"

"This evening," Mr Seacombe said. "Would you say the place was more like a library or a club?"

"A club. Which would be open to its members and visitors every day. Good. You do that, and I'll see what I can see at the man's place of business in Kaufingerstrasse. At least it's a busy street. A man like me finds it hard to hide behind lamp posts."

Well, perhaps they could be useful in their inquiries, after all, though Georgia hated to admit it. Louise invited the gentlemen and Marcus to stay for dinner, but they were already engaged with the ambassador at the embassy. They had also to see Millie back to the palace.

While Louise was busy with a *stadtplan* of Munich, spread out on the table so that she could point out the relative locations of the Society's premises and Bauer's place of business, Georgia took the opportunity to slip outside for a breath of fresh air. Marcus and Cora were no longer paddling by the lake, its only occupants now a half dozen swans and as many ducks. The scent of the chestnut spires was heavy on the early evening air, the smell of freshly mown grass a counterpoint to its sweetness.

"Do you see my boy?"

Her body may not have jumped, but her insides certainly did. She hoped he hadn't detected it.

"He and Cora are likely exercising their skill at *legerdemain* in the pantry."

With a chuckle, he said, "Feel like company?" Taking the lift of one shoulder as permission, he joined her in her slow promenade down to the water's edge. "You're angry with me."

How very observant. "Certainly not. Your comings and goings have nothing to do with me."

"You *are* angry."

She said nothing, merely watched the swans dabbling for food in the reeds.

"I've had some time to think, my lady."

There he went again, putting that oh-so-subtle caress on *my*.

"With an ocean and most of a continent between our homes, I should never have allowed myself to raise any expectations. For that, I'm sorry."

Raise expectations! Is that what he called it, with his admiring glances and his invitations to visit and his *my lady*?

"You give yourself too much credit, sir," she said coolly. "I have learned not to have any expectations of men at all. They are very rarely borne out."

Had he flinched? She hoped so.

"I don't blame you for your poor opinion of me. I had hoped we could be friends, after all we've experienced recently."

"That remains to be seen. For now, we have more important concerns."

He was silent. The ducks paddled over, looking up expectantly, but when Georgia showed them her empty hands, they turned away and contented themselves with harrowing the weed.

"Did you just communicate with those birds?"

"I merely showed them I had no bread today. Cora brought me down here to feed them the other morning before school. She is a day student at the Lycée des Jeunes Filles in town."

He was not to be distracted. "You seem to have a gift for communicating with creatures."

Georgia had never thought of it that way before. "I think it was the krakens who had the gift. They spoke to Millie, too, if you remember."

"Still. Most folks behave as though animals aren't there at all, or if they are, that their purpose is to be eaten or to serve. My horses would teach them different."

"They don't serve?"

A corner of his mouth quirked up. "It's more of a … negotiation." He sobered as he turned slightly toward her. "You're not really going to the archduke's lodge, are you?"

"I am. We must eliminate as many locations as we can from our list of possibilities. He does have the most to gain from her absence … or death."

"He also has a pretty colorful reputation."

"Mr Seacombe." Exasperation drove her to look him in the eye for the first time. "I was married nearly twenty years. There is nothing in the dissipation or cruelty of men I have not seen or experienced. I am no fainting ingenue who can be taken in by a title and a few roses. I am the sort of woman who can steal an airship, despite being shot at, and pilot it *alone* over the Alps to safety."

"I never said you—"

"I will thank you to give me credit for enough intelligence and courage to make my own decisions, to suffer the consequences of them if I must, and to raise or lower my *expectations* when and where I please."

The ducks had scattered. He rocked back on his heels as though a strong wind had come up over the lake. "I beg your pardon, ma'am."

She would never have dared to speak to Hartford this way. Aside from the inevitable blow had she tried, at that time she had had no accomplishments that would have bolstered her courage to speak. It felt rather good to do so, and more, to have a man acknowledge it. A man even more capable and courageous than she.

Though she was not about to let him know she thought so.

As they retraced their steps to the house, he spoke again. "Since my employer's plans have changed, and we will be doing what we can to assist you, may I request the honor of a dance at the Maifest Ball?"

She did have to consider it, though he probably thought she was pretending. "One dance," she said at last. "If I am to join the archduke's party and keep my eyes and ears open, I will not be able to break away so easily. The people here do not know we are acquainted. It would be best to keep it that way."

"I understand." He touched the rim of his hat and inclined his head, holding her gaze. "Until then, my lady."

Oh, how she wished he would not call her that!

The words were propriety itself. But what they did to her insides was the furthest thing from proper.

CHAPTER TEN

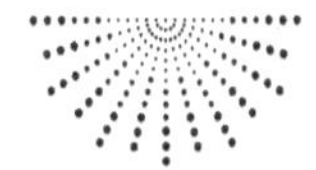

NYMPHENBURG

Friday, May 17, 1895
Midmorning

illie had hoped that her series of investigative triumphs might continue, but she had to concede she might have been overly optimistic. After breakfasting early, she had hastened up to the empress's private apartments, hoping to follow Johanna Fassmacher into the empress's bedchamber, or better, catch her in the act of dressing the automaton.

But when she arrived, slightly out of breath after climbing both curving staircases, she found the automaton already dressed and seated in the drawing room, for all the world as though it had been waiting for her.

There being nothing left to do but acknowledge its greeting, she curtseyed. "Good morning, Ma'am."

"I understand you have a message for me from the ambassador."

Goodness. She had completely forgotten that in her haste

to forestall the maids. "Yes, Ma'am." What could she say? Then she had it. "Mr Silverton wanted to inform you that there might be inquiries regarding the downing of his ship by air pirates off the Azores."

"Oh?" The destruction of ambassadorial vessels did not disturb its calm in the least. "What sort of inquiries?"

"They reported the crime in The Hague, but he felt your ministers ought to be made aware that the investigation is ongoing."

"I see. The Minister of Foreign Affairs was with him last night. It is strange that he did not convey this information to him directly."

Oh, dear. "I am sure he did, Ma'am, but they gave me the impression they wished you to be kept apprised as well."

The automaton nodded. "Very well. Thank you, Margravine. I have a task for you this morning."

Millie dared to seat herself on one of the spindly chairs. She opened the leather folder containing the schedule that had come by tube earlier, and pulled a small silver pencil from its loop. "Yes, Ma'am?"

"I fly to Linderhof this morning. Please reschedule my next four days' engagements."

Four days? What was it doing in the south for four days?

"Linderhof?" she said instead. "But Ma'am, I am informed that your ladies in waiting are returning this morning. Shall I send a pigeon instructing their ships to come about and wait for you?"

"Indeed not. I wish to work in my laboratory, and—I do beg your pardon—I need no one to attend me. You may not be aware, Margravine, that I go there frequently to work."

"But—but Ma'am, the Maifest Ball is tomorrow. Surely you will wish to attend."

"The Archduke Rupert will represent me," the automaton said serenely. "I much prefer working alone in the laboratory to dancing and festivity."

It sounded as though it was reciting information it had been given. But Millie had no way to know that for certain.

"You will fly all that way with no one to attend you?" she asked feebly.

"Johanna and Greta usually go with me. More than two maids are unnecessary, and they have already packed a few things suitable for work. You and my other ladies will go to the Maifest Ball if it pleases you, while I please myself in solitude at Linderhof."

Millie saw that they had reached a crossroads. The Landgräfin Winter was not the only one who would instantly realize the impostor in the beautifully made gown was not her royal lady. Ladies in waiting would not be bamboozled by a pair of maids into giving up their duties so easily.

The simple fact was that the ladies were all coming back in time for the ball—therefore the automaton must be removed from Nymphenburg on the most believable pretext in the world.

Someone was playing a shell game on a grand scale.

Millie did not give a fig whether the automaton was here, there, or in the Antipodes. Her task was to find the empress. Her only regret was that with Johanna Fassmacher going with it, she would not have a chance to find out who was giving the maid her instructions.

"When will you lift this morning, Ma'am?" she asked.

"Within the hour. I expect the captain will notify me that my ship is ready at any moment."

They would likely cross course with the ships bearing the ladies back to Munich. Would anyone remark on this backing and forthing? "Shall I stay here to reschedule your engagements, and listen for his tube?"

"No, thank you, Margravine. I am quite capable of doing so myself." It rose. "Good morning."

Dismissed, Millie could do nothing but curtsey and withdraw. Johanna Fassmacher and Greta passed her in the corridor, stepping aside and curtseying respectfully as she passed. Well. Good riddance to them. She had other fish to fry, so that with any luck, the morning would not be completely wasted.

She hurried into her own suite of rooms and found Lisabet brushing the walking costume she was to wear to attend the empress at the unveiling of a plaque in the Medicinal Gardens not far from the palace.

The girl turned in surprise. "Back so soon?"

"Her Imperial Majesty is going to Linderhof, and does not require me to attend her."

"Consider yourself lucky, ma'am. She might think she's alone there, but I feel sorry for her ladies and the maids, bored to death until she emerges from the laboratory demanding something to eat."

Millie had to smile. "You sound as though you have been there on such occasions."

"I have, ma'am. With Baroness Salzmann."

"It appears that Johanna and Greta are to go with her. I hope they are great readers and can enjoy the library."

Frowning, Lisabet turned away. Millie had the impression

she was not really seeing the walking costume on the rack before her.

"Lisabet? Is something the matter? You may speak freely with me. I have no one here to tell tales to, as you know, and honesty would be refreshing. Such a runaround as those two gave me last night!"

With this opening, Lisabet turned to face her. "That would be all of a piece. Greta is all right—too quiet by half. But that Johanna—" She rolled her eyes.

"She looks as though she ought to be in the army, striking terror into the hearts of new recruits."

A real smile flashed and was gone. "I heard she used to be a miner and that she's very strong. I wouldn't want to cross her, for true."

Strong enough to lift and manipulate an automaton made of metal? She'd been chosen carefully, then. "A miner? Heavens. What did she mine?"

"Well, she came with Baroness Salzmann, didn't she? The baroness's name says it all."

Salzmann ... salt man.

"The old baron's ancestor made his fortune mining salt four hundred years ago—and his heirs put in toll roads so that the merchants in their wagons coming to get it had to pay for the privilege. There are salt mines all through those mountains. The ones in Salzburg are the biggest, but there are any number of other ones, and the baron owns half a dozen of them."

Millie stored these facts away in case they should become more interesting than they were now. She returned to the topic at hand.

"I must write on the empress's behalf and reschedule her

appointments. Except for the Medicinal Gardens this morning—it is too late to cancel without causing offense. I shall keep that appointment. Thank you, Lisabet."

The girl smiled and returned to her work.

Millie uncapped her pen.

G—

Our mechanical friend is being sent posthaste to Linderhof attended by its two dressers. I suspect the return of the ladies in waiting this morning have precipitated its flight. Can you think of a way to find out who is giving the maids instructions? I feel as though our small circle is sadly understaffed.

M.

Millie sent off the tube to Kastanienhof and considered the royal schedule. She could only hope that the Margravine von Karlsrühe would lend the unveiling of the plaque at the Gardens enough gravity to soothe any ruffled feelings. There was a briefing after lunch that could be rescheduled easily, and then nothing until Monday, Dr Mainz having clearly assumed that the empress would be attending the Maifest Ball and would need all of Saturday in which to prepare. And of course Sunday was devoted to services ... and recovery from the night before.

She allowed Lisabet to dress her in the walking costume. The maid had arranged her hair earlier this morning in the braided crown that seemed to suit her so well. Her grey hat with its navy and rose ribbons certainly looked very becoming perched upon it instead of balancing unsteadily on her old pompadour.

Millie was pulling on the dusty-rose gloves she had

purchased in Venice when she heard the whoosh of a tube's arrival in the sitting room.

M—

Needs must where the devil drives. Cora and Marcus have volunteered for duty at Linderhof. L. will convey them there within the hour on the pretext of joining the empress in the laboratory, which I understand happens frequently enough that no one will remark upon it. She has also been charged with grilling the maids about their instructions. Knowing Louise, there will be no quarter given.

The gentlemen are coming to dinner to share what they gleaned today in their perambulations about town. Please come so that I am not entertaining them tout seul, *and stay a few days. With your mistress gone there is no reason for you to be knocking about there all alone. Better we stay together.*

G.

"Good heavens," Millie exclaimed. What a whirlwind Louise was, making such momentous decisions and acting upon them at the drop of a hat! And employing the children, too—mind you, that was only practical. If anything was to be discovered, it would likely be those two doing it.

Lisabet leaned in the doorway from the bedroom, where she was tidying up. "Is everything all right, ma'am?"

Millie collected her wits. "Yes indeed, thank you. I have been invited to stay with friends for a few days, since our royal lady will be absent. Would you be so kind as to pack all my things, Lisabet?"

"Certainly, ma'am." The girl grinned. "You have so little

with you it won't take above ten minutes. If you're going away, then I'll ask Dr Mainz if I might visit my family."

"An excellent idea. If he puts up any resistance, tell him you have my unqualified approval."

"I'll do that, ma'am. Thank you."

Millie had just enough time to reschedule the afternoon's briefing to the following week before the footman came to inform her the landau was waiting for her and the empress. Explaining the automaton's absence to the chauffeur was one thing—explaining it to the little committee and the audience of twenty or so at the Medicinal Gardens was quite another, and took all the grace and tact of which Millie was capable.

The committee, happily, possessed just as much tact, and were satisfied to have her read the prepared announcement, pull on the sheet to reveal the plaque, and then be accompanied around the Gardens for a tour of the medicinal plants growing there.

A frustrated gardener who had only really come into her own once Hartford was dead and could not forbid her pottering about in the roses and in the knot garden, Millie was keenly interested. She even asked several questions that gratified her hosts.

"And this one?" She pointed to a leafy plant with starry yellow flowers. "With a country name like Lady's Mantle, I assume this is for the treatment of female troubles?"

"You are perceptive, ma'am," the doctor leading the committee said. "Yes, the *Frauenmantel* is for the drying and tightening of the tissues and uterus following birth. It is also said that the Lady of Heaven's mantle offers protection for a woman at such a delicate time. Now, this one is the opposite." He indicated a cluster of leafy plants a little farther along the graveled path. "This was brought over from the Fifteen Colonies, where the first peoples call it *blue cohosh*."

Millie sounded out the syllables and pulled out her silver pencil to write down the name.

"It has been used by country apothecaries to induce labor, but I would not recommend it. We have at least two documented cases where people have stolen these plants to make a tincture, and found that the infants they hoped to welcome were born with heart failure."

"Good heavens," Millie said, shocked. She stepped away from the plants.

Considerate man that he seemed to be, the doctor ended the tour in a knot garden much like the one at Langford Park, only much larger and bedded with kitchen herbs from all over the world instead of flowers. She found herself filling the back of the royal schedule with notes. One never knew when one might get the opportunity to plant a few of these useful and interesting herbs.

Refreshed in spirit from being surrounded by plants instead of walls, and rejoicing in having made a few new friends among the committee, on her return to Nymphenburg she found that Lisabet had finished packing her traveling closet and her valise.

"Are you certain that you wish to take everything?" she asked, as Millie checked to see that nothing had been left behind. "It looks sad in here—as though you have gone home for good."

"With my friends," Millie confided, "one never knows whether one will be invited to tea, or on a jaunt to France in the airship, or to one of those odd progressive dinners where each household provides a different course. It is best to be prepared for anything—and to take everything."

Lisabet laughed. "Whereas I will be wearing castoffs and looking after my mother's chickens."

"When it comes to progressive dinners, I would much rather be in the barn talking to *die Hühner* myself," Millie said. "I will return when Her Imperial Majesty does, on Wednesday." She picked up her valise and grasped the handle of the traveling closet. "Good-bye for now, Lisabet."

"Goodness, ma'am, you mustn't take those out yourself. What would Dr Mainz say?"

"My dear child, I managed all this on the train from the north of the country. Walking out to the sweep is nothing." The first part was a fib, but it was true that the knack of managing her luggage was not new. When a woman was batted from household to household like a shuttlecock, she learned early to be efficient in packing and circumspect in moving.

Four days at Kastanienhof sounded heavenly. Lovely as Nymphenburg was from the outside, she thought as the landau bore her away, it was missing its heart. The sooner they located the young empress, the better.

CHAPTER ELEVEN

LINDERHOF

Friday, May 17, 1895
Midafternoon

Mama brought in *Thetis* as gently as a petal falling to the grass, and Cora and Marcus ran down the gangway to help Emil and the ground crew with the mooring irons.

"Hullo, back already?" Emil greeted her.

She introduced Marcus, then said, "Yes, Mama has invented some new part or something and she can't wait to share it with the empress."

Emil laughed. "Just like always. You go on—we'll take good care of faithful *Thetis* here."

"They should," Marcus murmured as they ran under *Sisi*'s swelling fuselage and joined Mama on the straight gravel path up to the palace. "There's only our two ships on the field."

"The ladies have all gone back to Munich. But you're right—it isn't often you see it so empty."

"Good for us, if we're going to do a bit of spying." He grinned, and all his freckles seemed to dance at the prospect.

"I expect you both to be discreet," Mama said over her shoulder as they climbed the left-hand set of the graceful omega shape the stairs formed up to the great double doors. "Keep your eyes and ears open, and if you get a chance to ask a pertinent question, don't hesitate. Just remember—"

"Know the nearest exit," she and Marcus chorused together.

The butler directed Mama into the laboratory while he went to announce her to the empress. Before he'd fairly got his back turned, Cora had dragged Marcus through the green baize door that led downstairs under the grand interior staircase. They found Anya in front of the enormous cooking range, tasting something simmering in a pot.

"Hullo, I didn't expect to see you today. Try this—is it salty enough?"

Cora tasted it, and then offered the rest of the spoonful to Marcus. "Mm, mushroom soup. It tastes wonderful. Is that for lunch?"

"*Ja*, for us below stairs. The empress will take a tray in her suite. Are you here with your aunties again?"

"No, with Mama. She is keeping the empress company in the laboratory."

"Herr Bach says our royal lady will not stop here long."

"It's lucky we came today, then." Cora glanced at Marcus, who looked as puzzled as she felt. With people of rank, *not stopping long* could mean an hour or a week. "Is she to visit someone else?"

"Burg Salzweg is all I heard." With two towels, Anya picked

up the wide pot by its handles and took it over to the head of the scrubbed table where the staff had their meals.

"What's Burg Salzweg?" Marcus whispered. "It sounds like one of those desserts made of marzipan."

"I don't know, but Mama will. Come on, let's have some of that soup."

The soup was the best she'd ever eaten, and that was saying something. The crusty bread and thick wheels of creamy cheese, accompanied by cold steamed spears of white asparagus with a tasty sauce, made up the rest of a truly satisfying meal.

When Herr Bach the butler rose, signifying it was time for everyone to return to work, Cora whispered, "I'll stay here and talk to Anya. You have a look round the palace and see what you can see. We'll meet back in the laboratory with Mama."

He went out with two of the footmen, who took no notice of him, while she found a towel to help Anya with the dishes amid the mad clatter of the cook and her assistants. "No scullery maid today?"

"She's got a cold—conveniently coming down with it just as all the ladies left this morning." Anya sniffed with disdain. "I'm glad you're here—it took me all morning to wash the breakfast dishes. The empress and your ma won't be nearly as much trouble as that lot."

"Never mind, it seems you'll be down to no one at all soon, if *Sisi* lifts."

"Is your ma not staying?"

"I don't think so. She only came to bring a part ... or talk over some new invention. I forget. I don't care—as long as I don't have to be at lessons."

"*I'd* like to be at lessons," Anya said with a sigh, submerging half a dozen soup bowls and setting to scrubbing. "But my mother can't afford the lost wages. And I can get ahead here in the palace, where I couldn't in the village."

Cora felt sorry she'd said anything so silly, when Anya would have loved what she pretended not to like.

"Have the ladies been a trial?" Better to change the subject. "I suppose the ladies have ladies' maids, do they?"

"Oh, yes. It's a military operation getting them all fed, let me tell you. When the empress is here with them, we run from dawn till dark—later, if there's a ball. But there hasn't been one of those in ages, thank goodness."

"The Maifest Ball is tomorrow in Munich," Cora said. "I think Mama and my aunties are going. My one auntie is going to open the dancing with Archduke Rupert."

"Is she now?" Anya looked impressed, lining up the bowls on the counter for Cora to dry. "I'd like to see it someday. What a sight it must be, with all the ladies in jewels and the gentlemen waltzing."

"You might come home with us and see it," Cora said impulsively. "Mama won't mind, and it's nothing to bring you back the next day."

The dreaminess faded from Anya's face and she addressed herself to the next set of soup bowls. "I can't. Even if our royals and ladies aren't in residence, the staff is here year round. They still have to be fed and the dishes still have to be done. We don't get paid, you know, for days we don't work."

"No, I suppose not. Forgive me."

Anya smiled. "Speaking of the archduke, want to hear some gossip?"

"Oh, yes." Cora never missed a chance for gossip. She

might not understand all of it, but it was always interesting, and sometimes even useful.

"Well, Frau Bach the housekeeper was upstairs the other day, standing by, you know, in case any of the ladies needed anything. One of them got a tube from her husband, who waits on the archduke. He said Rupert was in love again, and they had to hunt through all the palaces' greenhouses to find enough red roses to send her. They're not in season in regular gardens, of course."

Cora had a sudden realization. "Three dozen red roses?"

"I don't know how many, but it was an awful lot."

She whispered, "The lady he sent them to is my auntie. She can't stand him."

"But you said she's opening the ball with him," Anya whispered back, shocked.

"Wouldn't you?" She didn't dare mention *why* Auntie Georgia had accepted his offer.

Anya had to admit that she probably would dance with him, if she got the chance, which was all nonsense, since she was only twelve. "The lady in waiting was reading the letter out, you know, so that all of them could hear. I wonder if her husband knows she does that. Anyway, he said the archduke had better enjoy the dance, since there's talk of finding a wife for him from one of the Nordic royal families."

"I'm sure he will enjoy it," Cora said loyally. "My auntie is a very good dancer." She hadn't seen her dance, not really, but Auntie Georgia was very graceful and that was as good as. "When is the empress getting married, do you think?"

Anya snorted. "I suppose she could marry her cousin, but if I was her, I sure wouldn't. He's down here once in a while with all his herd of gentlemen, drinking and carousing and dropping their cigar ash in the carpets. The mother's helpers can't keep up."

"If he was married, he'd have to stop all that."

"If he married Empress Christina, he'd be emperor, and wouldn't have to, would he?"

Cora supposed that was true, but she felt a little sorry for Christina, in that case.

"A bunch of his gentlemen were out in the garden, smoking, one night a few weeks ago, when she wasn't here. One of them even said that if she said no, she should have her crown taken away and given to the archduke."

"Nobody can do that," Cora scoffed. "Once you've been crowned, you are whatever majesty you are until you die."

Anya shrugged. "I only know what I heard him say."

Cora stored this up to tell Marcus, and then it was time to do the pots, and that was too much work to talk. What seemed like a long time later, she said good-bye to Anya and took a short cut to the laboratory via one of the corridors the footmen didn't use so often, because the empress didn't allow food and drink in there.

Footsteps were coming toward her at a dead run.

Out of habit, she stepped into a recess. It was a stroke of luck that it held a rack of unused livery. She concealed herself behind it.

The footsteps skidded on the rough sisal of the floor runner, and in two seconds she had company in her niche. Company she knew as well as her own reflection in a mirror.

"Marcus," she hissed. He yelped and she grabbed him before he could leap headlong into the corridor to flee. "It's me—Cora!"

He let out a great breath. "The automaton is coming with the maids. I hope they didn't see me."

His whisper had barely evaporated when not three feet away, a woman said, "Listen to me, Christina."

Cora stood on tiptoe and peeked over the livery's shoulders just in time to see two women in grey dresses and white aprons accompany the automaton down the corridor. The uniform of the royal attendants at Nymphenburg.

"If anyone is so impertinent as to ask, we are going to Burg Salzweg to persuade Baron and Lady Salzmann to return to court."

"Yes, of course," the automaton said.

Burg Salzweg again. What was so important there that the automaton had to visit, pretending to be the empress? Cora grabbed Marcus's hand, and together they slipped out of hiding to follow them. Thank goodness the corridor was dim. Their quarry turned left, which would lead them to the gardener's door under the formal stairs outside.

"How funny the empress's maids should take her out this way," she whispered. "Aren't these the ones dressing it and fooling everybody?"

"But the truth is," the maid went on as she reached the door, "that you are going to stay there for a few days."

"I shall be away four days," the automaton said, as though it was agreeing.

"And all this business will be over by then. Your task will be ended."

"My task will be ended. Now I shall return to the laboratory. I know Lady Thorne well."

"No, Christina." The maid opened the outer door, and

Cora and Marcus ran to catch up. "You will board your ship now. You are not to be touched."

"I am not to be touched. Thank you, Johanna. Greta, please go on ahead and notify the captain to set his course for Burg Salzweg. We lift immediately."

Oh, goodness. Clearly *not stopping long* meant not even one afternoon!

"What did it mean about its task being over?" Marcus whispered.

"Something is happening down at Burg Salzweg," she replied. "They asked the automaton to lie about why it was going there. We need to find out."

Clearly the automaton was being spirited out of the palace like the machine it was, not the empress it was supposed to be.

"No one is supposed to know, seems like," Marcus agreed. "I don't have as much spy experience as you, but even I know that the things grownups aren't supposed to know mean serious business."

They ducked out of the gardener's door and slipped through the herbaceous border, which luckily contained tall hollyhocks, not short primroses. Their concealment wasn't the best, but still they followed the automaton and the maid she called Johanna, the other one being halfway down the avenue already to tell the captain they were coming. Cora pulled Marcus through a laurel hedge, and once they were properly out of sight, they began to run. After covering several hundred yards well ahead of the pair, they hid behind a tree a stone's throw from *Sisi* to take stock.

"Where is Emil?" she panted. She had just moments.

Ducking under the fuselage, she spotted him at the starboard mooring iron with one of the lieutenants. He saluted smartly and rapidly gave the ground crew their instructions.

"Quick, into the communications cage!"

"Are you mad?" Marcus squeaked. Had he forgotten they were supposed to be spies? "We have to tell your mother!"

"No time—here, I'll give you a boost. Go!"

She boosted him into the pigeon chute, and he scrambled up the way he had showed her on *Foresight*, back on the island in the Venetian lagoon. Well, *Sisi* wasn't as big as that, but it would still allow him to get in—and her, too, in a minute.

Cora pelted the considerable length of *Sisi*'s fuselage, staying well out of sight of the flight crew in the gondola.

"Emil!" She grabbed his arm as he jogged past to the stern irons.

"Can't chat, the empress is lifting."

"I know, I'm going with her. Tell my mother when she comes down, will you?"

"You're going with her?" He goggled at her. "What for?"

"Because I speak four languages, silly." She rolled her eyes for effect. "The empress has asked for me personally because I am useful *sometimes*, you know. We're going to Burg Salzweg, all right? Tell my mother that."

"All right, Miss Fancy Translator. I'll tell her."

"Give me a boost into the communications cage?"

"You can go in by the gangway. If you're crew, you're allowed."

"No time! She's practically boarding now. Come on, *schnell!*"

He made a stirrup with his hands and boosted her up into the pigeon chute. She scrambled up as fast as she could, and at the top, Marcus hauled her into the cage. They both went over backward with an "Oomph!" when the bow of the ship dipped with the automaton's arrival.

And a minute after that, as the two of them lay staring at the ceiling, panting and trying to recover from their mad dash down the entire park, the teak deck pressed up under Cora's back.

They were falling up into the sky, and there was no going back now, even if they wanted to.

CHAPTER TWELVE

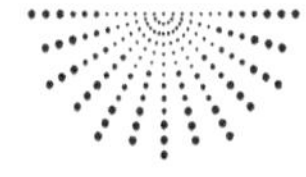

KASTANIENHOF

Friday, May 17, 1895
6:20 p.m.

Not to be outdone by mere archdukes, when they arrived for dinner, Mr van Meere brought Millie a bouquet of freesia, fresh from a flower stand in the Victualienmarkt.

Millie buried her nose in the yellow, cream, and orange flowers and breathed them in. "How lovely they are! We shall enjoy their scent all through the house."

"We will as soon as these roses are removed." Georgia instructed Mrs Brucker, Louise's housekeeper, to carry the massive bouquet downstairs and distribute them among the staff with her compliments.

Then she led the way into the drawing room to hear how the gentlemen's day had gone, until dinner should be announced.

"So Lady Thorne is not at home this evening?" Mr

Seacombe settled in the armchair, while Georgia and Millie took one sofa and Mr van Meere the other.

Georgia exchanged a glance with Millie and Mr Seacombe caught it. "It seems awful quiet around here. Have Marcus and Cora gone somewhere, too?"

"You could say that," Georgia said. *Dear me, how awkward.* "Please understand that there was not time to wait until you arrived this evening, and of course there was no way to know where exactly you were in town in order to ask permission."

"The automaton has gone to Linderhof, and Louise and the children followed it," Millie said bluntly, since Georgia's information did not seem to have enlightened them.

"Marcus is at Linderhof?" Mr Seacombe looked astonished, then amused. Had Georgia received similar information about Teddy, amusement would not have been her reaction. But then, perhaps that was only a matter of luck and circumstance. Marcus and Teddy would likely become fast friends were they ever to meet, so similar were their minds. "He will enjoy that. But I thought all the ladies in waiting were returning today, for the ball. Will they stay now, and miss it?"

"They are already returned," Millie said. "Therefore, to prevent anyone other than Landgräfin Winter realizing the automaton has taken the empress's place, whoever has concocted this plot has removed it to safety. It is a shell game, and the automaton is the prize."

"I'd very much like to know what they've done with the real prize," Mr van Meere growled.

"Do tell us about your inquiries at the Technical Philosophical Society," Millie said. "I managed to accomplish nothing useful but unveiling a plaque and touring the Medicinal Gardens. Oh, and warning Louise that the automaton was about to be extracted."

"It was Louise's idea to set Marcus and Cora loose in Linderhof," Georgia explained, still feeling a little guilty that they had removed Marcus from his father so high-handedly. "I do not know if she will reveal herself to the automaton and its keepers, or stay aboard *Thetis* and wait for the children to report in."

"Unlikely, that last, if I know Louise," Mr van Meere said. "If she behaves as though it's the real empress, no one will bat an eye. They're always together down there, tinkering with this and that."

"Which is what she said. Now, what happened on your side?"

"I spent a good hour hanging about Fritz Bauer's business premises," Mr van Meere began, "to no avail. The staff came and went, but he did not. Finally I went in and pretended I had an appointment. I was told, of course, that there must be some mistake, that he was in a meeting of the Technical Philosophical Society." He rolled his eyes. "So I drove over there and decided that as long as Seacombe remained incognito, I was safe enough in revealing myself. Bauer's staff would no doubt tell him I was asking after him, so it would look odd if I didn't."

"The meeting was odd enough to begin with," Mr Seacombe said. "The subject under discussion, if you can believe it, was salt."

"Salt?" Millie leaned forward. "How strange. I learned a few tidbits about Baroness Salzmann's family this very morning. The baron, it seems, owns half a dozen salt mines. And the automaton's dresser, Johanna Fassmacher, was once a salt miner before she rose to her present position in the palace."

"There was a Fassmacher in the meeting," Mr Seacombe said thoughtfully. "Man in his early forties, maybe? Favored his right leg. Eyes the color of an ocean in bad weather."

"That cannot be a coincidence," Millie said at once. She turned to Georgia. "Johanna's eyes are the grey of those ball bearings Teddy used for marbles as a boy."

"Any number of people here have grey eyes, or blue eyes, and blond hair," Georgia said, striving for impartiality. "We cannot make assumptions based on that. But why were they talking about salt? What technical philosophy could possibly cover something one sprinkles on food?"

"Not its use—its extraction. Mining machinery," Mr van Meere said. "Fritz Bauer recognized me right away and welcomed me to their discussion like a man with nothing on his conscience, introducing me to everyone—"

"Even me," said Mr Seacombe, one corner of his mouth twitching. "I was using my English identity and accent, so they didn't make uncomfortable connections. But strangely, once Cornelius joined us, the talk drifted away from mining machinery and on to some new airship Zeppelin just introduced."

"The LZ-48?" Georgia asked. "That was the one I toured the other day."

"The same." Well, goodness, he didn't need to look so surprised that she knew its model number. "What did you think of it?" he asked.

"It was very comfortable—and despite its size, it is designed so that it can be flown by a full crew, or by one person. All the equipment in the gondola, for instance, is on movable trusses and tracks so that it can be pulled within arm's reach if needed. The galley is constructed under the same principle."

"Galleys are usually constructed for one person," Mr Seacombe said. "Except *Foresight*, and then only if Monsieur LePine permits someone else to help him."

"Have you ever produced tea for twenty in a ship's galley?" Georgia asked rather tartly.

"Can't say I have."

"Countess von Zeppelin did, to prove it could be done." Georgia tilted her chin and returned her attention to Mr van Meere. "Why do you suppose they left off talking about salt mines when you arrived? Did they suppose the subject would hold no interest for you?"

"That I couldn't say," he admitted. "I'd have been very interested, from what Seacombe says."

Mr Seacombe's thoughtful contemplation of her face ended as he nodded to his employer. "Before Cornelius arrived, they were talking about a new machinery design one of the engineers had read of. Speculating about its use for transport of the salt from the deepest horizons of the mines. Some of the largest have forty miles of tunnels in almost inaccessible mountains."

"Where did he read of it?" Millie asked.

"It was a monograph by an engineer in the Texican Territory, as it happens, and this man was giving his opinion."

"Written by Mr van Meere?" Millie asked, not sounding very surprised.

"No, by a witch name of Yang May Lin."

"A *witch*?" Georgia blurted, shocked at his language. "Is that what they call female engineers in this country?"

The corner of his mouth quirked up. "It's what they call the *brujas* of the river canyons on the borders of the Royal Kingdom of Spain and the Californias and the Texican Territory. Those women are the most feared individuals in the Wild West—and this one in particular has invented a kind of machine that can scale sheer cliffs on articulated legs. Which becomes interesting to mine owners like Baron Salzmann, who are looking for more efficient methods not only to get the crystals out of the rock, but then to transport them to a railway, road, or river barge."

"Baron Salzmann?" Millie said. "His name actually came up?"

"Yep."

Georgia frowned, and not because of irritation with Mr Seacombe and his possible connection with fearsome women in the Wild West, either. "Does it occur to you all that an alarming number of coincidences are piling up?"

Millie held up a hand and bent down the thumb. "Baroness Salzmann realizes she is expecting a child that may or may not be the baron's, and goes home to the family pile."

"The empress is abducted and the last person known to have spoken to her—her possible abductor—is Fritz Bauer of the Technical Philosophical Society," Georgia said. A forefinger.

"The baroness accidentally leaves a torn-up note in her desk telling the recipient to *take to your burrow and hide in the dark with the others*. Which could be construed as a mine if one were so inclined." Millie bent her middle finger. "One of the automaton's dressers is a former miner." The fourth finger.

"And she shares a surname with a man in said Philosophical Society," Georgia finished, as the smallest finger bent. "I have changed my mind on that point."

Millie lowered her closed fist.

"That is a heap of coincidences," Mr van Meere agreed after a moment. "And here's another oddity—why didn't the Society members ask me what I knew of Yang May Lin? They may not know we are acquainted, but they know I hail from the Texican Territories. If they're thinking of brokering a deal between a mine owner and an engineer with technology, I'd be the most likely person to ask for assistance. But instead, they changed the subject."

"Unless they were planning to invent their own machine using the monograph," Mr Seacombe pointed out. "Which is illegal, if she's got a patent on it."

"That I don't know. It just seems odd they didn't ride the trail all the way home, is all."

"It is odd," Georgia agreed. "But now, here is Mr Brucker."

Standing in the archway to the dining room, the butler bowed. "Dinner is served, Lady Langford, *en famille*, as you requested."

There was nothing for it but to go in on Mr Seacombe's arm, and sit beside him at Louise's table without benefit of butler or footmen. Somehow this seemed more intimate than it had even in Venice, where they had eaten at the same table many times. Perhaps it was because Mr van Meere had declared his intentions toward Millie, and was at this moment pouring wine for her with infinite care. And here they were on the other side of the table, the undeclared and, on her part at least, the disinterested.

Very much disinterested.

She took up the conversation where it had left off. "If we

were to discover that any or all of these Philosophical people or the miners are connected with Archduke Rupert, I should be convinced of a plot," she said. "But honestly, what do miners and machines from the other side of the world have to do with the empress? The simplest solution is often the best—that her disappearance can be laid at her cousin's door."

"Coincidence is not the same as cause," Mr van Meere said, nodding. "But it shouldn't be dismissed, either."

"If Lady Thorne and the children come back with additional coincidences, they might change the picture." Mr Seacombe helped himself to the venison steaks with pepper sauce. "May I?"

Upon her inclination of the head, he slid a steak onto Georgia's plate. She took up the tongs and put some white asparagus next to it, then passed him both tongs and platter. The sauce boat followed. In no case was she going to perform such a wifely act as serving him in return. No, indeed.

"Louise and the children have been away nearly all day," she said, taking the potatoes Chantilly from Millie. "I do hope we will hear from them soon."

"Or better yet, see them," Mr Seacombe said, his voice as low as a growl.

Thirty minutes later, with a *whoosh* a tube dropped into the communications cabinet set into the wall. Georgia put down her dessert fork. "I hope that is from Louise. I am becoming quite worried. They were not meant to be away this long." When she returned to the dining room, having skimmed the contents, she was not able to meet Mr Seacombe's eyes. Instead, she took a deep breath and read the note aloud.

"G—

By the time you get this, I will be in the Bavarian Alps, or nearly. For reasons known only to themselves, the children boarded Sisi, the empress's airship. I am told Cora is to be the empress's translator. The ship's course is set for Burg Salzweg, the seat of Baron and Lady Salzmann."

"What in tarnation?" Marcus's father demanded.

"Good heavens!" Millie exclaimed.

"*That* is no coincidence," Mr van Meere concluded grimly.

"Since I have allowed people to think the automaton has fooled me, I cannot understand why its handlers have removed it from Linderhof. Something very odd is going on, which clearly the children understand better than I. When I find them, I will send a pigeon to Foresight. Sending even this much by tube poses a risk.

In haste—

L."

"Mr Seacombe, I am certain that nothing dreadful will happen to Marcus and Cora," Millie said, touching the clenched fist that lay on the table.

"If it does, the son of a gun who hurts him will regret it."

Georgia gathered her fear into a ball and shoved it away. "If anyone is capable of avoiding trouble while soaking up information, it is Marcus and Cora. Louise will find them, you may depend upon it."

Mr Seacombe looked as though she had dealt him such an insult he would have thrown down the gauntlet had he possessed one. He rose from his chair like a thundercloud in the west. "Do you think, ma'am, that I am going to leave it to someone else to locate my boy and make sure he is safe?"

Ma'am spoken in that tone might as well have been a glove across her cheek.

"Louise must be there by now," she said, bearing up under this indignity. "Do you consider her abilities less than yours, after she eluded two governments and a ring of assassins to reach Cora the last time?"

"Georgia." Millie's voice held both gentleness and a warning.

"I respect that woman's abilities more than you know, having been acquainted longer," came the whiplash of a reply. "He is my son, and I am going. Cornelius, if *Foresight* is not available, I'll go on the train."

"What, now?"

"This moment."

"Seacombe, no one can sneak up on anything in *Foresight*," Mr van Meere said. "She's too big for any private landing field. You might as well bring an army and announce yourself with a fusillade of cannon."

"The train it is, then. You'll forgive me if I borrow the landau." He snatched up his Stetson from the table in the foyer and before Georgia could even catch her breath, the door closed behind him with a thud.

"For goodness sake, Cornelius, go after him!" Millie cried. "You cannot let him go off half-cocked."

"Dustin Seacombe never goes anywhere half-cocked." Mr van Meere strode out of the dining room. "We will all go together. Fetch your valises, ladies. You have ten minutes."

Millie hurried up the stairs, Georgia on her heels.

"Millie, stop! They cannot go on *Foresight*—you heard what he said. The Salzmanns would see that massive ship coming ten miles off."

"I don't expect we are. I expect we will *all* take the train. What a lucky thing I brought all my things from the palace. Shall you travel in your flight clothes? That seems most— Georgia?"

For she had come to a halt in the middle of the carpeted corridor. "I cannot go," Georgia said, feeling once more as though she had been struck. Only this time it was recollection that had landed the blow.

"What do you mean? This is urgent. We must go help Louise. What if Cora is in danger?"

"That is just it. I must do something less dangerous, but equally urgent—attend the bloody wretched ball tomorrow. Open the dancing with the archduke. And then be invited to his hunting lodge so that I can search it from attic to cellar."

"But my dear—"

"I can't go flying off across Bavaria with you. Not when we have such a chance to infiltrate a location where Christina might be."

Millie leaned against the wall as though it might hold her up. "Then I am staying with you. We will go to the ball together. And then I shall go to the lodge, as your chaperone."

The thought of dear, fragile, brave Millie in that house of Dionysus was enough to make Georgia recoil in horror. "Dearest, I have not had a chaperone since I married your nephew."

Millie was recovering now, and pushed herself upright once more. "Perhaps not. But if you are the chosen companion of the archduke, you *will* need a lady's maid. He has never seen me, nor, I hope, have any of the gentlemen with him. If one of them has spotted the Margravine attending the empress, I am not sure what I will do, but I will think of something. Be a twin sister, perhaps. We will go to the ball, go to the lodge, and once we are certain Christina is not there, return to Nymphenburg. From there, the Margravine von Karlsrühe and her companion will take one of the palace airships to Burg Salzweg, having been sent for by the empress."

Georgia tried not to gape at her. "My word, but you are quick on your feet."

Millie smiled a little ruefully. "My time at the palace was brief, but my feet have never moved so quickly, nor under so much duress. Listen—there is the door. That will be Cornelius. We must tell him what we mean to do."

If ever two men felt trapped between a rock and a hard place, it was their two friends when Millie and Georgia explained the change in their plans. But Mr Seacombe, having the most at stake, gained the upper hand.

"You may stay, Cornelius, and do what you think is right. I am going to find my boy."

He climbed into the pilot's chair of the van Meere landau, and at this usurpation of all that was holy and good, Mr van Meere wrenched up the wing and waved him into the navigator's seat.

His eyes were worried as he took one last look at Millie on the step. "You will be all right? Promise me."

"I have survived drunken routs before this, and sneaking about in royal residences. I will be quite safe. Good-bye for now, Cor—Mr van Meere."

He might have come over to kiss her hand, but from inside, Mr Seacombe said something Georgia could not hear. "Until we meet again," he said at last to them both, and climbed in.

Moments later, gravel spat under the landau's large rear wheels, and they puttered down the avenue to vanish in the twilight created by the hour and the chestnut trees.

Once again, Georgia reflected, Mr Seacombe had departed without a good-bye. But this time she did not have the heart to blame him for it.

8:45 p.m.

Cornelius lumbered down the corridor to check *Foresight*'s communications cage while Dustin went to the cabin that was his and Marcus's second home. He changed swiftly out of his dinner clothes into practical dungarees, a chambray shirt, and a waistcoat with a hidden pocket containing a folding knife more discreet than his Bowie. With efficient movements born of experience, he checked that his six-shooter had bullets in each chamber, plus a few in his belt pouch to spare, and strapped on his gun belt. After shrugging into his caped leather coat, he filled his rucksack with some food and stuffed in Marcus's wool jacket. Up there in the Bavarian Alps, it would still be cold, and the numpty had taken off in only his shirtsleeves.

"Dustin." Cornelius stood in the doorway, holding out a piece of notepaper and looking grim.

Cornelius—

 As it turns out, the imperial mechanics did not quite obey Christi-

na's charge to repair Thetis. Our trips to Linderhof have exacerbated a problem I did not see in time. I have gone down on the banks of the lake, just north of Bernau am Chiemsee, to which I walked to find a mechanic. I have been able to procure parts, but they cannot be delivered before morning, no matter how high my inducement. Night is falling so, much as it irritates me, I admit I cannot begin the repairs, plus those incurred in the landing, until tomorrow in any case.

Shocked, Dustin looked up. "Louise doesn't say if she's injured."

"Doesn't sound like it, if she walked into town." Van Meere's eyes were grave. "What are the odds she gets to Burg Salzweg at all?"

"I'm not willing to lay those odds." He returned his attention to the note.

Do not bring <u>Foresight</u> to rescue me and frighten half the country. Do not be alarmed for Marcus and Cora, either. I will fly to Burg Salzweg to discover them as soon as I can lift again.

    Louise

Dustin handed the note back to Cornelius. "Doesn't change my plans."

"Nor mine," his employer said, heading to his own cabin to change. His voice drifted down the carpeted corridor. "Bernau am Chiemsee is on the train route to Salzburg. We'll disembark there, help her with the repairs, and fly to Burg Salzweg with her in *Thetis*."

Now *that* was a sound plan. Dustin felt the tight coil of anxiety in his chest loosen a little.

Foresight's bosun doubled as chauffeur on the rare occasions when Cornelius was willing to surrender the pilot's chair. The man dropped them at Munich's train station, a soaring vision of iron and glass that was filled with a miasma of steam as the last trains prepared to depart. Cornelius, wielding money like magic, procured a first-class compartment on the eastbound train, which would pass Bernau a couple of hours before dawn.

"Best get some shut-eye," he rumbled, sliding open the compartment door as the whistle screamed and the train lurched into motion.

Before Dustin could so much as snort at the impossibility of such a thing, a voice hailed them from an adjoining compartment.

"Van Meere! What are you doing here? Don't say you're invited down to the castle too?"

Across the corridor, Fritz Bauer leaped for the open door to seize Cornelius's hand and pump it.

"And Seacombe! Don't you look like you strolled straight out of the Texican Territory." He captured Dustin's hand in a grip of iron. "Are you playacting?"

"Not I," he said in his usual Texican accents. "I'm a man of two countries. This is the other one. Mr van Meere and I ran into each other at the *Hauptbahnhof* and discovered we shared a destination."

Bauer laughed, as though this were particularly clever of him. "You didn't say a word at the club."

"Neither did you," Cornelius pointed out. He waved the man and his three companions into his considerably larger and more comfortably appointed compartment. It even had a sofa, and a closet with a discreet sign indicating its personal nature to boot.

"Best to keep some things close," Bauer said. "To be honest, I'm not sure whether I'm more intrigued or frightened, even if we have been waiting for such a summons."

"You? Frightened?" one of the other men said in disbelief. "That's no attitude to go on with an empire at stake."

The man next to him gave him an elbow in the side so sharp that he had to muffle a cry. "We're in public, you dolt."

"We're also among friends," Cornelius assured them, indicating the closed compartment door. "Mr Seacombe, as you know, is a man of parts and keenly interested in my activities here. He's also handy in a scrap, aren't you, Seacombe?"

Dustin chose to respond not with any theatrics of firearms, but with an enigmatic smile as he put a hand on his hip, moving his coat aside oh so slightly to reveal the six-gun in its holster.

"I'd trust him with my life," Cornelius concluded. It was the truth, and he paid Dustin handsomely for that confidence.

Their very real friendship was a bonus.

The compartment door slid open to reveal a waiter, who bowed and asked for their orders. Since dinner at Kastanienhof had been what seemed like hours ago, Dustin ordered another one. Best to fill the belly while you could, because you never knew what lay around the corner. Bottles of fine French brandy and good Bavarian Andechs beer appeared, and under their benign influence, conversation began to flow as freely as any babbling brook.

No one seemed to notice that the levels in the Texicans' glasses did not seem to change much, and if they did notice, they dismissed it in gratitude for the cheerful liberality of their host.

While Cornelius did his part in disarming them and gaining their trust, Dustin set aside his usual taciturnity and employed his skill at drawing information out of their unexpected guests. *The castle* could only mean Burg Salzweg. In which case, burning in his mind was a question for which his concern for Marcus and their friends demanded an answer. He danced around it for the time it took to dispose of a bottle of brandy, and when dinner was concluded and Cornelius opened the second, Dustin moved in for the *coup de grâce*.

"Bauer, my friend, how long have you been involved in all this?" he asked, his glass dangling from his fingers. "A man of your skills must be in demand."

Bauer smiled modestly. "I always leaned toward republican ideals, especially at university. Hans here, was in my engineering classes then. He knows."

"All too true," Hans said, nodding wisely. "We've been underground a long while."

"But it wasn't until the old Emperor announced that Christina would be his heir that I suddenly saw the future, like a vision. That woman belongs with us. She's wasted as empress. Making small talk with diplomats and opening schools?" He snorted. "Ridiculous."

"And your vision became reality." Dustin sounded thoughtful.

"It wasn't until the baroness got involved that the royal derailment began to pick up speed. It's not that we're traitors to the empire, mind you." He pointed at Dustin, who was not offended.

"Of course not. But..."

"But the empire is blessed with intelligence in its women."

"Beauty, too." One of the others whistled.

"It doesn't hurt," Bauer said. "The baroness will become a widow soon, and marry the archduke. She's already carrying his child, contrary to what that old stick of a baron so fondly believes. Christina will see sense and abdicate, probably with great relief. The baroness is one of us, and with us managing her, and her managing that buffoon—"

"Now, Fritz. He's a good sport," Hans protested. "Been hunting with him a time or two, and those parties—" He rolled his eyes and whistled. "Legendary."

"The man will die in his cups, leaving the empire to his lovely widow, the Empress Regent, holding the throne for their son."

"Or daughter," Cornelius put in, filling the man's glass.

"We'll hope for a son, and deal with a daughter." Bauer took a sip. "Family's a little short on boys. Dashed Mecklenburg bloodline. If we have to, we can always build another automaton."

The elegant compartment rocked with laughter.

When it settled, Hans was looking pretty owlish. "Haven't quite figured out how we'll make Christina see sense, though."

Bauer sighed, rolling his eyes in Dustin's direction as though looking for his agreement about the man's stupidity. "Dear boy, it's likely she's seen the light already. She's a mechanic. Practical. She never really took to her role, merely played it competently. And if her stay at Burg Salzweg doesn't convince her, then we'll have to take more dramatic steps."

"I heard she was at Linderhof," Dustin said, the picture of confusion.

Another gale of laughter.

"You were meant to hear that," Hans said, nodding, and once begun, seemed unable to stop. "Automaton's dashed convincing. *Nein*, she's been at Burg Salg—Salz—with the baroness all this time."

"Hence this gathering of friends." Dustin gazed at them, with the grin of a conspirator. "I'm looking forward to this."

Hans revived, casting around for his empty glass. Dustin considerately filled it. "Only one problem." Hans took a sip. "Two problems."

Bauer gave a snort, buried in his own glass. "One isn't a problem at all. His love affairs last five minutes. Our lovely Emma will make short work of her."

Dustin was not entirely pretending confusion now, as he looked from one to the other. "Whose love affairs?"

"Rupert's, of course," said one of the others, shaking his head. "He made a spectacle of himself over her at the Zeppelin works. Granted, the lady's a stunner. But no more than the last one. Or the one before that. With a bun in the oven, our Emma doesn't care for competition."

"Oh, that one." It was an effort for Dustin to appear relaxed. "I heard she was opening the ball with him tomorrow."

"Ooh." Bauer winced. "That will set off our little firebrand's temper. It was supposed to be her, until she was called home."

"*Sent* home, you mean," the other man said, snickering. "Christina presides over the most prudish court in a hundred years."

"The new *amour* is far away, though," Dustin said over the pounding of his heart. "Not much our lady can do from the castle walls except curse."

More laughter, of which Dustin was becoming very tired. "I'd be surprised if there wasn't a Famiglia Rosa coin already in play," Bauer chortled.

Assassins. Once a coin was given, the assigned murder was carried out no matter how much time it took. Minutes. Months. Years.

Dustin's heart seemed to freeze in his chest.

CHAPTER THIRTEEN

SALZWEG

Saturday, May 18, 1895
Before dawn

The good thing about traveling in the communications cage was that you could communicate. Yesterday, Cora had wasted no time in sending one of *Sisi's* pigeons to *Thetis*, for she had no doubt her mother would be watching for it.

Dear Mama—

Those two grim maids have spirited the automaton out of Linderhof and are taking it somewhere called Burg Salzweg. Castle Salt Way? Castle on the salt road? A peculiar name.

I hope you are not worried. We are both well. We will try to find out what they are doing before you come.

Love,

Cora and Marcus

That was yesterday, and Mama had *not* come. Cora did not

know whether to be terrified or pleased at Mama's confidence in them. Had something happened to her? Should they wait for her aboard *Sisi*? Or should they find their way somehow into the castle without being spotted, and do the job they had come to do?

In the end, as first the ship's passengers and then the crew disembarked and yesterday had faded into twilight, two priorities floated to the top: food and somewhere safe to sleep.

"If Mama is coming," Cora had said in the end to Marcus, "she will have to moor here, and we will hear the engines at least, no matter how late."

Marcus had nodded. "If we go up there now, she won't know where to find us, even if we sent another pigeon. When we don't know the lay of the land, it's best for the three of us to stick together. And your mama, I know, is very good at finding a way up things." He had gazed up at the terrible precipice upon which the castle was built, hundreds of feet high. "Even that."

Cora couldn't imagine how they could have built anything up there where nothing else lived but eagles. Maybe they'd carved the place out of the living rock. She's heard that expression once—the living rock. It was not a substance you thought of as being alive, because what did dead rock look like? But here they were, faced with a castle set on top of a mountain that was sheer on one side and normally sloped, with forests and every-thing, on the other. Far below was a town, clustered around two broad, well-kept roads that were likely the ones the castle had been named for. The airfield was about a quarter mile from the outskirts of the town.

Getting that far wouldn't be a problem. Getting up that mountain would.

So they had raided the galley of the royal vessel for their dinner, being as tidy as they knew how to be. The empress probably employed the last word in chefs, and with Marcus's experience with Monsieur LePine, they did not want to get on the wrong side of him. Then they'd found an unoccupied stateroom and curled up together in the sleeping cupboard.

Cora had awakened while it was still dark and tiptoed across to the viewing port. In the east, the sky was turning grey along the serrated tops of the Bavarian Alps. On the far side was Salzburg in the kingdom of Österreich. When she returned to the cupboard, Marcus was awake, too. They made the bed quickly, washed their faces and hands, and raided the galley for food they could take with them—a small round cheese, two apples, and a quantity of nuts that Marcus said would sustain them for quite a while in a pinch.

Cora didn't want to consider what kind of pinch he meant. Still, she filled the pockets of her dress with them just in case.

It was likely that *Sisi* lay under the keen eyes of the airfield's night watch, so they disembarked via the pigeons' chute, landing in the dewy grass and losing a number of nuts in the process. As they zigzagged across the field, under cover of three other airships, they met no one.

They did not see *Thetis*, either.

"Where is Mama?" she demanded of the silent fields. As they walked down the road, its surface lightened to a visible grey under the waning half moon.

"Maybe she didn't get the pigeon," Marcus replied. "Or maybe *Thetis* had mechanical difficulties."

Cora opened her mouth to say both possibilities were

ridiculous. But maybe they weren't. "The empress's engineers repaired her. The real empress promised. And we've been flying back and forth to Linderhof already."

They gazed at each other, Cora's own trepidation mirrored in Marcus's eyes. "What should we do?" he said at last. "We can't come all this way with nothing to show for it."

Cora made up her mind. They could still do something. And in doing it, beat back the terror brought on by visions of *Thetis* going down on a glacier, or in a lake.

"We stick to the plan," she said, trying to iron the wobble out of her voice. "Find out why the automaton is here, and search the castle for the real empress, the way Auntie Georgia will search Archduke Rupert's hunting lodge tonight."

Marcus nodded, and wasted no more time. "Come on, then. It's getting lighter by the second."

By the time they covered the quarter mile to town, lights were glimmering on in people's houses. Light or no, Cora had to admit she didn't notice much of the town. Not after she'd had an eyeful of the funiculars.

"We have to go up in one of those?" Marcus breathed.

From this angle, they had a view of the mining operation that had not been visible from the airfield. On the far side of the river, barges and train carriages waited empty, while iron carts full of salt crystals trundled back and forth from the bases of the funiculars to docks and platforms. Above, in the growing daylight, they could see more than one level in more than one mountain, if the mine openings where tracks came out and met the funiculars were any indication. Each cart hooked onto a vertical apparatus that took it down, where it was unhooked, unloaded on a waiting barge or train car, then reattached and sent upward once more.

"They're like enormous moving ladders," Marcus said.

"They're ugly," Cora said flatly. "They're spoiling the entire valley."

"Not for people who like to look at money," Marcus pointed out. "Anyhow, we don't want to go to the mines. We want the castle."

"Surely we don't have to walk all the way around that mountain to find a road." Cora felt exhausted at the very thought. It was miles, surely. "They wouldn't make the empress do that, or the lord and lady either. There must be a way up for guests coming by airship."

"They can't make their company walk all that way when they come for dinner," Marcus said by way of agreement. "I suppose we'd best not ask, though."

"I'd say not. Have you any German?"

"Just a few phrases. *Good day* and *thank you* and such."

"If we do need to ask, let me do the talking. At least I have a Bavarian accent. That will help. For now, let's see what we can see."

Any hope of assaulting the mountain in darkness was now melting away as the glow over the eastern peaks intensified, turning the snow to gold. In a moment the sun would burst out from behind those peaks, and with it, the promise of a warm day. At the moment, though, Cora wished she had thought to bring a coat, but they had expected to be home yesterday by sunset, so there had seemed to be no need for one.

She should have known better. A spy ought to be prepared with more than her school cardigan. Never mind. She must make up for that oversight by coming up with a plan.

"Cora, what's that?" Marcus pointed. "All the trees have

been cut down in a straight line, right the way up the mountain."

"Another mine?"

"No, it's all by itself. Do you suppose that's the way up to the castle?"

The cut lay well away from the shout and clank of the funiculars. "It could be. Maybe they don't want to listen to the racket of the mining equipment that's making them all their money."

"I guess we'd better look. At least that road there has a bridge. Come on."

No one accosted them on the bridge, which was becoming busier. A whistle blew, and a few minutes later a flood of dusty, salt-encrusted men crossed the bridge on foot while a flood of clean ones came down from the town. In the melee, no one noticed a pair of children veer to the east and walk through the forest on a gravelled road.

"This has to be the way," Cora panted. "They lay down gravel at home so the landaus' wheels don't get stuck in the mud."

It felt like a long walk, trying not to be seen on the grassy verge of the road and listening every second for the crunch of gravel that would tell them someone was coming. But eventually they came to a broad sweep, where there were several landaus neatly lined up at the foot of a private funicular.

"Look!" She grabbed Marcus's arm. "That's the royal landau. From *Sisi*. See the crest on the wing?"

The tension in his face relaxed. "So far, so good. The only thing now is ... where is a carriage to take us up there?"

Oh, dear.

Perplexed, Cora gazed up the narrow mechanical ladder

that sliced through the forested sides of the mountain. Up and up … until her head was tilted back. "I can't see anything. Is there only one carriage? If they took the automaton up in it, is it sitting at the top waiting for them to bring it back down?"

Marcus groaned. "Maybe there's a bell."

She snorted. "Ring the bell of the house you plan to burgle?"

"They don't have to know it's us. We can jump out of the carriage before we get all the way to the top."

"It can't hurt to look, I suppose."

Checking about them carefully, they made their way between the landaus to the foot of the funicular, which terminated in an engine house that lay silent. Marcus crossed to the steam engine that powered it, and laid a hand on the iron cowl.

"Cold. No one's gone up since last night." Silently, they gazed up the funicular until it disappeared into the heights. "Someone has to come and start the engine, but that could be days. We might have to climb that thing, like a ladder."

He couldn't be serious. "It's a long way to fall," Cora said. "Seven hundred feet at least. It's nearly vertical on some of those cliff faces."

"It might be our only choice."

Cora had no fear of heights, but any goose could see that they'd fall off from exhaustion before they even got halfway. "The winding grease will make those cogs slippery. We'd likely lose a hand or foot into the bargain if the carriage started down. Too risky."

"Here's the bell. I think." An apparatus that resembled nothing so much as the dumb-waiter at Linderhof was set into a niche in the rock. It was the size of a cupboard that might hold a couple of bags of flour, and on the floor was a pad of paper and a pencil, presumably to send a message requesting the carriage to whoever was at the top. "Look. Release this latch and the thing goes up. It's on a tension system of pulleys."

"I suppose this is where the milk is delivered?" Cora was only half serious. "I wonder if it goes to the kitchens?"

Marcus considered the aperture. "Never mind the milk—do you think it will hold both of us?"

Saturday, May 18, 1895
Kastanienhof, 3:00 p.m.

The longest day in the history of time had finally passed—endless hours in which Georgia's mind could only circle around the whereabouts of the children and Louise—and wonder whether or not Mr van Meere and Mr Seacombe had reached their destination. It was a relief when the clocks at last chimed the hour at which Georgia and Millie could begin dressing for the ball. It was to begin in the late afternoon, as it was a public festival, and end, she supposed, when the provisions ran out.

But she would have departed long before that. She hoped.

"I must pull out all the stops to guarantee an invitation to the lodge." Georgia held up the sapphire ballgown whose low neckline had so offended Queen Margherita di Savoia in Venice.

"That will certainly do it," Millie said. "Will you wear the sapphires, too?"

"I suppose I must. If one opens a ball with the heir to the

throne, one must commit to it completely, tiara and all. You'll wear the pearls?"

"No indeed."

Georgia turned in surprise.

"If I am to be your companion, I must be the woman who trailed behind you at our first audience with the automaton. Dressed in grey, dowdy hair, and so likely to blend in with the wallpaper that she is instantly forgotten. I must present as great a contrast as possible with the Margravine von Karlsrühe, so that people do not connect the two."

"You are quite right. Please tell me you plan to dance, at least."

Millie shook her head. "I shall be a wallflower, sitting somewhere poorly lit with the other chaperones."

"And picking up what gossip you may?"

"Of course." Millie smiled like a girl, and Georgia saw that she actually possessed a dimple. One might almost think skulduggery agreed with her.

So Georgia donned her battle dress, complete with the Langford sapphire parure and sixteen-button kid gloves that extended nearly to the shoulder, while Millie put on a silvery grey dress that was so proper and out of date it screamed *maiden aunt*. She did not do her hair in the braided crown, but rather wore it low on her neck—a style she had worn when she'd first come to Langford Park. There, the deeper the friendship had grown between the two women, the higher her hair had been dressed, as though she was becoming less afraid to occupy her own space.

But tonight, Georgia was to shine, and Millie was to return to her old habit of invisibility. It was a lucky thing Mr van Meere was not to accompany them, for he would not understand why Millie could not shine with the best of them. But they could not afford for anyone to recognize her as the Margravine. Frankly, Georgia hardly did herself, and they had helped each other dress.

The archduke had sent an old-fashioned horse-drawn carriage to convey them to Nymphenburg. She was grateful for that, only because it meant the Kastanienhof chauffeur was now free to join the rest of the staff among the celebrating citizenry. This was no society ball in some duchess's stuffy ballroom, Georgia saw at once as they passed through the main doors of the palace and were directed straight through to the enormous courtyard on the other side. This was a city-wide celebration, where anyone who wanted to might dance, eat, and drink.

"Do not lose me," Georgia begged as they descended the white marble steps. "It is like Vauxhall Gardens, only twice as large."

"Little likelihood of that," Millie said wryly. "You will be the most visible woman here. Speaking of, your escort approaches."

She faded back a little way, leaving Georgia to extend her gloved hand to Archduke Rupert, who was busy taking her in as though she were a succulent fruit pastry on a plate.

"My dear Lady Langford." He kissed the back of her glove, straightened, and tucked her hand into his elbow, covering it with his other hand. "The festivities may commence, since the evening star has now blossomed on the horizon."

"I am no Venus, Your Grace," she murmured modestly, catching the allusion.

"I must beg to contradict you ... my Venus, my Aphrodite, my heart's own queen."

For how many hours must she put up with this? But Georgia only smiled. Should she be as remote as that star, or as earthy as the goddess for which it was named? Perhaps modesty was the best course between these two extremes. He was a hunter. Very well, her virtue would lead him a merry chase through thickets of difficulty until she could escape to do what she'd come to do.

When the archduke led her to the exact center of the enormous courtyard, the orchestra played the *Kaiserhymne*—the national anthem. When it concluded, one of his attendants stepped forward with a speaking horn and presented it to him.

"Citizens of Munich," Rupert boomed cheerfully. "We celebrate the close of another Parliament and I, representing Her Imperial Majesty Empress Christina of Prussia, now have the pleasure of welcoming you all to Nymphenburg. Tonight we meet old friends and dance until dawn. Strike up the orchestra and let the festivities commence!"

Georgia practically had to run to keep up at his side as he made for the expanse where the sets were forming. No wonder the man was so popular. No long, windy speeches for him, just a hearty welcome and straight to the dancing. And like the Prussians—organized to a fault—there were at least a dozen sets of two dozen couples each already forming, laid out in military formation across the lawns and gravel walks of the massive courtyard.

She felt the gaze of everyone in the lead set as he escorted her to the top, the speculation so heavy that she was obliged to lift her chin to counteract it. Whispers ran like a wind through the crowd, and those in the sets farthest away craned their necks for a better view.

To her relief, the archduke was a competent dancer, though as the evening progressed, each time his man approached her to tell her that her company was desired, she found him slightly more unsteady on his feet. She, on the other hand, limited herself to one glass of wine and a small portion of the food laid out on long tables. For one, her corset was laced just tightly enough to show off her figure to advantage, which did not allow for gluttony. And for another, her nerves were thrumming to the point that if she overindulged, she might be sick.

Millie found her periodically throughout the evening.

"Surely you are dancing just a little?" Georgia asked her as they sought out the ladies' withdrawing room.

"In the lower sets," Millie confessed. "There, it is unlikely anyone will recognize the margravine. How are you holding up?"

"I have yet to secure that invitation, but believe me, I will."

"The gossip about your identity is rampant."

"I am sure it is. Speculation lies like a fog upon the company."

"I'm told those roses you received were the result of the looting of every royal hothouse within a ten-mile radius."

"Poor roses, to lose their lives in vain."

"They say he will propose by the end of the evening. That you are some Norse princess and come with a dowry of two castles and four provinces."

Georgia laughed. "Little do they know I have nothing but the clothes I stand up in and what my son is kind enough to give me—and I am more content with that than any castle."

Two hours later, they met again to marvel at a golden automaton shaped like a swan that had been carried out and placed in the middle of the dessert table. Each time it preened its brass feathers, a chocolate egg rolled out on the tablecloth, to be snatched up by a lucky onlooker.

Millie was quick. She shared the egg with Georgia. It was beyond delicious, and had a cream center the color of a yolk.

"Here is your dance partner," Millie murmured. "It is after midnight. Perhaps you may yet receive an offer that would make your mother faint."

"Let us hope so. I am beginning to wish for my comfortable flight boots. These slippers were a poor choice for out of doors."

Georgia held out her hand to Archduke Rupert and was escorted back to the dancing. A barely perceptible edging separated this gravel walk from the lawn, but his toe managed to find it. When he drunkenly regained his balance, she took a chance. "Perhaps, sir, we might sit this one out, and enjoy the sight of so many enjoying themselves?"

"Good idea." He waved a hand, and the family occupying a nearby bench fled, bowing with every step.

"Sir," she said reproachfully. "That was hardly necessary. There are many benches."

"When my lady wishes to rest, her wish is my command. And this bench is well lit. I can gaze at you to my heart's content. Mind you, I can't do what I'd like to do were it behind a hedge."

"Certainly not," she said, the primness of her tone contrasting with the bat of her lashes.

"How have we endured a lifetime without meeting before?" His eyelids were beginning to droop, along with his gaze, which seemed unable to leave her decollètage.

"We make our homes in different countries." She seized

the opening. "It is true I have not had the honor of seeing you here as much as I might like. Nor have I had the pleasure of seeing your home."

"We must remedy that—indeed we must!" He straightened as though this idea had never occurred to him.

"What is it like, sir? I picture it in a forest, with all the heads of the beasts you have killed mounted on the walls." *How revolting.*

"You are a seer as well as a goddess. That is exactly what it is like. And you shall see it this very night."

"How shall I do that? Isn't it very far away?"

"Not half an hour in the landau. I will show you over the place and you may tell me that you wish to live there with me forever."

She gave a tinkling laugh. "In that case, we may need to negotiate the animal heads."

"My queen will command, and it shall be done. Holbein!" he shouted.

The factotum who arranged the archduke's dance partners appeared out of thin air. "Sir?"

"Lady Langford wishes to see the royal lodge. Round up my courtiers. We go at once."

"Very good, sir."

Before he could fade into the crowd, Georgia called, "Mr Holbein, if you could let my maid know that I will require her, she can travel with us. She is there by the punchbowl, in the grey dress with the lace collar."

He bowed. "Certainly, ma'am."

The archduke looked at her owlishly. "Your maid is coming with us?"

"Of course, sir. Your gentlemen are coming with you, are they not? Gentlemen of the bedchamber and whatnot?"

"Of course. Bedchamber." He chortled. "Naughty minx. We're in public."

"I shall require her, sir," she said with meaningful emphasis. Let him make of that what he would. She would do her best to avoid going alone into any bedchamber with him. To always be in company.

Every other room in the house, however, was fair game. She and Millie would definitely manage that alone.

Saturday, May 18, 1895
10:45 p.m.

Georgia and Millie's conveyance to the lodge was a six-piston Benz landau, a mechanical triumph that would have made Teddy swoon merely to behold it. Georgia had the presence of mind to make landaus the subject of their conversation on the way, since along with Millie on the rearmost bench, two of the archduke's gentlemen rode with them. She was quite pleased by her ability to hold her own, especially when the topic turned to piloting such a vehicle. By the time they passed between the tall, mossy posts of Hirschfeld, named, Rupert informed her, for the fields in which the deer once liked to graze, they were all fast friends.

"Once?" she inquired of him with a twinkle. "Have you shot them all?"

The gentlemen laughed. "Almost," the archduke said. "We have to range farther afield now—sometimes as much as a day on horseback. The canny animals know better than to get within range of either arrow or bullet."

The chauffeur pulled up in the sweep and Rupert handed her out first, before the rest of the gentlemen tumbled out like so many puppies. Millie, she noticed, took the navigator's chair and began to converse with the chauffeur as the landau pulled away.

Clever Millie. For they should need a way back into the city from the depths of this forest, and making a friend in such a position might help to accomplish that.

The archduke lost no time in plying Georgia with drink in the massive barrel-vaulted feasting hall, which was the main feature of the ground floor. Tasting her wine, she repressed a shudder at her surroundings. The place was a baronial fantasy, full of animal heads and dark green or oxblood painted walls, except for a mural of the hunt painted twenty feet high at the far end, behind a dais whose dining table and chairs were carved with as much detail as a cuckoo clock. Overstuffed sofas were arranged in clusters, and at the near end was a fireplace in which the proverbial ox could be roasted. The dogs underfoot were healthy and friendly, though wet noses and doggy kisses did not pair so well with silk. When one of the gentlemen called them away, and she begged her host for a tour of the house.

"In a hurry to see the upstairs, are we, my queen? No wish of yours shall wait for an instant. Come. Let me show you all."

It did not take long to see the rest of the ground floor, which consisted of a drawing room where, presumably, any ladies might find some peace and quiet, the kitchens, the steward's offices, and the usual pantries and storerooms. In the interests of being thorough, she peeked into each one, frightening a maid and offending a butler in the process.

The archduke found this hilarious.

To her relief, the door to the kitchen opened to admit the chauffeur and Millie, who thanked him and hastened close enough to hear if she were called for.

"Is this the cellar door?" Georgia asked, trying the handle near a pantry the size of a bedchamber. It opened just enough to tell her it was not habitually kept locked. Millie, she saw, noted its location, her face calm and disinterested.

"It is," Rupert said, pleased at her attention. "Even better, there is a sub-cellar where they used to keep armaments for defense. And I hear there is an escape route—a tunnel to the river."

"Is there?" What a good place to keep a woman you wanted out of the way. "Have you ever escaped that way yourself?"

He laughed. "Despite the occasional irate husband, I've never had to use it." His gentlemen joined him in raucous humor. "Now for the upstairs, as soon as someone gets me another drink."

Someone soon obliged. As Georgia and the archduke climbed the ornately carved stairs—really, was no piece of wood safe from chisel and knife here?—one by one the gentlemen dropped away and returned to their own pursuits in the great hall.

Excellent. Fewer witnesses.

There were twelve bedrooms and a solar upstairs, and she looked into each one, remarking on hangings and peeping into trunks and closets—even the occupied ones. Rupert tolerated her impossible nosiness with patience, presumably counting his indulgence the price of his eventual reward. For it seemed he was saving the royal bedchamber for last.

"Is there more?" she asked. "I would love to see the attics. So romantic and ghostly, aren't they?"

"Nothing up there but servants' quarters." His face, flushed with drink, managed a puzzled expression. "No attics here. I say, you are an extraordinary woman. Come along now, enough of this. I want to show you the peece—the piss—"

"The *pièce de resistance?*"

"*Ja.* My rooms. This way."

A chorus of laughter echoed up the staircase, and he relaxed back into good humor. Flinging open a door carved within an inch of its life with what appeared to be an imperial eagle, he ushered her inside. She barely had time to flash a *Don't leave me* message to Millie, standing discreetly at a distance.

The room was twice as large as the others, tapestry bed hangings descending from a frame half the size of a cottage. Pillows trimmed in handmade lace were piled at the head, and the velvet coverlet was invitingly turned back. A dressing gown lay draped over the foot. Three sets of floor-to-ceiling French windows marched along one wall, leading to—

Of all the unexpected things to find in a chamber of seduction. "Do you collect these, sir?"

A herd of rocking horses in many shapes and sizes occupied the corner between windows and fireplace, from one that might be ridden by a toddler to a life-sized one with a sneer to its upper lip, as though disdainful of any rider but royalty.

"Mine, yes. Like 'em?"

"They are wonderful." It was the first sincere remark she had made all evening. "My son had one very similar to this." A dappled grey with a tail of real horsehair rocked gently at her touch. "I haven't the heart to put it away, so it sits in his room even yet, though he is up at Oxford."

"I hear that out in the Tex'can Terr'tries, they have mechanical horses. Use 'em in battle. I've sent fer one. Must add it to the c'lection."

The collection? Had he not ridden them himself, as a child? "Heavens. Better that, I suppose, than to send highly trained animals to their deaths."

But evidently the time for polite conversation had ended, and foolishly, she had allowed herself to be distracted by the rocking horses. For now he stood between her and the still-open door.

"C'mere, Queen Georgia. Give us a kiss."

"Sir!" Georgia spread one hand over the sapphires, the picture of offended modesty.

"What's yer objection? Yer in m'bedroom, aren't you?"

"You are showing me your house. I had no idea you had ulterior motives."

"*Ja*, you did. You don't fool me."

"I have no intention of fool—"

He grabbed her around the waist and attempted to plant a wet kiss on her mouth.

But she had not suffered such drunken embraces for so many years for nothing. One foot slipped behind his, a twist, a push—

The archduke landed flat on his back on the bed. The feather mattress fluffed up around him and impeded his movements just enough that with a rustle of silk, she made it to the door. Before she laid her hand upon the knob, she was startled by the sound of a snore. Even with that assurance, she floated down the staircase with more speed than grace, to meet Millie hovering in the grand entrance hall.

"We are leaving?" the latter inquired hopefully.

"Not yet. We must check the cellars. There is a tunnel."

The two of them returned to the now silent kitchens and passed through the door Georgia had remarked on before. A basin full of moonglobes was attached to the wall at the landing, so they each took one and shook it into life. The cellars were vast—clearly once meant for the processing of stag and boar for the court. Even the light of the moonglobes could not reach into the corners, or behind looming piles of crates and bags of flour and potatoes that testified as to the appetites of the present heir and his gentlemen.

"Where is the door?" Millie whispered, circling the rooms like a maddened moth. "The tunnel is supposed to go to the river, you say? How far?"

"On which side of the house?" Georgia forced herself to stop and take stock of her location. Stairs, front entrance, drive… "We passed a river on the way in, did we not? One of the gentlemen pointed it out. It must run behind the house. In that case—" She did an about face. "Check these storage rooms."

In the middle one, at last, they found a door. "I do hope it is not locked," Millie murmured. "If one were keeping an empress in a tunnel, one would lock the door, no?"

The latch depressed under Georgia's hand. "If your logic holds, then we are chasing wild geese, not empresses."

"Still, we must be certain."

The tunnel was rounded and lined with bricks. It lay, arrow straight, with hardly a root or stone underfoot, as though it were regularly used and kept in good repair.

As they walked, Georgia said, "Were you making arrangements with the chauffeur for our transportation back to Kastanienhof?"

In the bluish glow of the moonglobe, Millie's eyes were shadowed. "I made a valiant attempt, but the archduke's instructions were that all parties were staying the night. The chauffeur has gone home. He did tell me that there is to be a grand breakfast and then riding in the morning."

"What, in this?" Georgia indicated her silk skirts.

"Evidently the plans of gentlemen do not take a lady's changes of clothes into account. When I said as much, he was rather nonplussed. But he would not stay. We shall be forced to steal that monster of a landau, or beg a lift from a kind person passing on the road. It is a good ten miles back to town—and the middle of the night to boot."

"Stealing is preferable to walking ten miles in these heeled slippers."

"My dear, your morals have sunk indeed since you stole *Thetis*."

"I know," Georgia admitted cheerfully. "I assaulted the heir to the throne just now, too. The drunken buffoon deserves to have his landau stolen."

The tunnel ended at another door, which opened as easily as the first. The cool night air blew past them, ruffling Georgia's hair, and they heard the chuckling of water. After climbing a set of stone steps, they found themselves on a stone pier jutting out into the river. In the light of the waning moon, a curious kind of vessel bumped against the bladders that lined the stone, clearly meant to prevent damage to it.

"Another wonder for Teddy," Georgia murmured. "He said in a letter he would be racing aquapedes at Cowes. I couldn't imagine what such a thing would look like. I wonder if this is one?"

The vessel seated two, one behind the other. Slender

paddle wheels on each gunwale appeared to be powered by the feet of the forward person, who sat in the pilot's chair, while the rearmost person had the tiller.

Georgia eyed the direction of the current.

Millie elbowed her in her corseted ribs. "You will not steal the aquapede and add to all your other crimes."

"I do not see that we have a choice, unless we sleep in the barn or walk for the rest of the night. The river will flow into the Isar, which will take us straight into Munich."

"And how are you going to return it?"

"I shall send your friend the chauffeur a tube advising him where he may find it," Georgia said. "We must move on to the second part of your plan, dearest. It is clear the empress is not concealed here. We must join Louise in the morning as the margravine and her daughter."

"This morning, you mean."

"But for the moment, we have only one decision to make."

"I," Millie said instantly and very firmly, "am *not* going to do the paddling."

CHAPTER FOURTEEN

SALZWEG

Sunday, May 19, 1895
10:05 a.m.

The smallest of the royal fleet of airships sank gently to the grass, to be swiftly moored by the ground crew, and the Margravine von Karlsrühe and her daughter disembarked. They were dressed in clothes suitable for flight, even to the daughter's flight boots and her ladyship's goggles perched upon her hat. The lady must be a little absentminded, for she did not remove the latter, simply picked up her reticule and boarded the landau awaiting them courtesy of Baron Salzmann.

"What a stunning view," the margravine remarked as the landau rumbled over the bridge and the scope of the mining operation became visible. "Does the baron manage the mines himself?"

The chauffeur nodded. "Some in the village say they're his in name only, but I know for a fact that he likes to keep his hand in. No dust on the baron, no sir—ma'am."

"The empress was likely fascinated by the funiculars," her daughter ventured. "At least, Mama tells me she is very mechanically minded."

"That she is," the chauffeur agreed, piloting them down a gravel road. The trees leaned close, nearly blocking what sunlight managed to make it past the shoulders and peaks of the mountains. "Not on this visit, mind, but on previous ones she's escaped the company and been found talking with the mine managers and getting private tours. The baroness has been none too pleased on those occasions, with company invited up especially to be presented." The landau came to a stop at the foot of a precipice, broken only by a funicular stretching up and up. "Here we are, Margravine. If it pleases you to enter the carriage, it will take you up to the castle courtyard."

Her ladyship gazed upward, a tiny frown marring her brow. "Up there? In that? Alone?"

"It's quite safe, ma'am. The salt goes up and down on these all day and all night. Only twice in ten years have we had a break, and only once was a man lost."

"Oh, dear," her daughter said faintly. "Come, Mama. Her Imperial Majesty is waiting. Duty demands courage."

A good philosophy, if ever the chauffeur had heard one.

He led them to the carriage, handed them in and made sure they knew where the overhead straps were located, then touched his cap and went around to increase the pressure on the steam engine. While it came up to full, he loaded a crate from off the airship into the kitchen closet, which rose swiftly out of sight with its burden. When the whistle on the engine blew, he worked the levers and the carriage lurched into motion.

. . .

GEORGIA FLAILED and caught a ceiling strap with one hand and Millie with the other. "My word," Georgia gasped. "How fast it travels." The engine house and the row of landaus dwindled to the size of a child's toys, then vanished altogether. Under the metal floor, she could hear the cogs engaging and releasing, thrusting them up the mountain with great energy.

"I don't like this at all," Millie said through her teeth, gripping a strap with both hands. "How is it that I can fly in an airship without fear, but this thing has me rooted to the floor with terror? I refuse to look out of the viewing port. I shall be ill."

"Try not to, dearest," Georgia said, watching the forward port closely. "We seem to be arriving."

The carriage clanked into its housing and she barely remembered her role in time to allow Millie to precede her, then followed her out looking as meek as a spinster daughter ought. Feeling as shaken as she did certainly contributed to the effect.

A man and a woman stepped forward to greet them, a couple of men in frock coats and traveling gear behind them. If she were a gambling woman, she would say they were engineers. How, she could not say, but a slight disregard for one's dress and fingers spotted with stains of winding grease were usually good signs, if Teddy could be used as a measure.

The man in front was nearer seventy than sixty, formally dressed in a black coat, brocade vest, and perfectly cut trousers. A strap going diagonally across his head held a leather eye patch in place. He bowed to Millie.

"Margravine von Karlsrühe," he said. "I am Baron Gunther Salzmann. Welcome to our home."

"Thank you, Baron," Millie said, rising admirably to the occasion now that it was clear he had never met the real margravine. "The approach to your house is, er … striking."

He smiled, and Georgia found herself liking the remaining eye's twinkle and sincerity.

"May I present my daughter, Georgia, who accompanied me in lieu of my maid." He bowed over her hand as Millie went on, "She does not have much opportunity to travel, so I hope you will forgive the imposition."

"It is no imposition at all. May I introduce my wife, Baroness Emma Salzmann."

Georgia took in the baroness as she curtseyed to Millie. Not yet thirty, she'd estimate, with curly blonde hair and the china-plate blue eyes that were so popular nowadays. Her lips were red and full, her cheeks pink as apples, and her figure was exactly what Georgia had learned the Archduke favored, with the added glow of pregnancy.

"We are delighted, Margravine—and Fraulein von Karl-srühe," she said in a little-girl voice that did not match the intelligence in those eyes. Georgia curtseyed to her, as rank dictated. "Please, do come in. I will introduce you to all this rabble over a welcome cup. We keep the old traditions here."

She smiled at the four men waiting behind them, who surrounded her like a litter of puppies. The baron offered Millie his arm and escorted her across the courtyard into a baronial stone hall that still held the chill of winter. Georgia followed, taking in the stone heights and crenellations, to say nothing of the enormous rose window over the double arched doors. Had this building once been a church, built as close to heaven as earthbound men could achieve?

In a medieval solar hung with dusty-smelling tapestries, another handful of men waited, glasses in hand, one regaling the others with the tale of losing two of their companions.

"Vanished in the night, they did," he said, his glass tilting dangerously. "But they'll turn up for the meeting, I'll be bound."

Another poured brandy and wine while Georgia and Millie settled opposite the baroness on velvet-upholstered sofas with wooden backs that had probably been constructed when the Tinkering Prince had ascended England's throne.

"I am afraid I have bad news for you, after you have come all this way," the baroness said, offering Millie a glass of wine from the tray one of the gentlemen presented. "Thank you, Fritz."

Georgia froze in the act of accepting her wine. Fritz? Could this be the Fritz Bauer whom Mr van Meere and Mr Seacombe had met at the Technical Philosophical Society? Why were the gentlemen not being introduced if they were on such familiar footing with their hosts?

"Goodness," Millie said, taking a sip. "My word, this wine is delicious, even so early in the day."

"Thank you." The baron smiled rather proudly. "Another of my pursuits—a vineyard on the Moselle."

"If the salt mines ever fail, your future career is assured."

The man actually lost color. "Margravine, I see I shall have to work to keep up with your sense of humor. We never refer to the mines in such terms. The one time my great-grandfather made such a mistake, a man died in an accident."

Now it was Millie's turn to pale. "I do beg your pardon. I

hope the bad news you have for us is not connected in any way with my carelessness?"

"No indeed," the baroness said smoothly while her husband recovered his composure. "It is only that your royal mistress has already departed. She left this morning, before our friends here arrived, having inspected the mines yesterday."

Georgia's mouth dropped open just a little, and she closed it hastily.

Millie leaned forward. "But I was to attend her during her visit. I came immediately I learned that she had left Linderhof and requested *Sisi*'s course be set for Burg Salzweg. The empress must be attended by one of her own ladies when she visits, no matter how well staffed a home might be." She smiled apologetically at the couple, so that they would not be offended. "I do not understand."

"You are very new to Her Imperial Majesty's service," the baroness said, laying a comforting hand on Millie's knee. Removing it, she went on, "Perhaps in everything you have had to learn so quickly, you forget that I, too, am one of her ladies in waiting, though I have been obliged to return home while I await our child." She smiled fondly at the Baron, who seemed dazzled by her show of affection. "I was able to offer all the services she required, having been familiar with them for some time."

"Oh," Millie said, flustered and blushing. "I am so sorry, Baroness, I did not mean to imply—I am, of course, your temporary replacement, and—"

"Think nothing of it." The young woman waved her guest's consternation away.

But Millie could not be soothed. "We will trespass upon

your hospitality no longer. I am so sorry—to come all this way with hardly any notice when you have company already—"

"Mama," Georgia said in a low tone, "calm yourself. The baron and baroness would not think of begrudging hospitality to anyone. Would another sip of wine help your nerves?"

"Thank you, dear," Millie whispered, taking an obedient mouthful.

Georgia caught the amused glance the baroness sent one of the engineers, and resisted the urge to tip her own glass down the woman's silken bosom. How dared the vulgar woman so embarrass a guest in her husband's home?

"It is out of the question that you should fly back to Munich so soon," the baron said with the kindness of a true gentleman. "We are hosting a meeting this afternoon of the Technical Philosophical Society, of which I am proud to say my wife is a member. Two more ladies at dinner will be a most welcome addition."

"Hear, hear," said another of the engineers, raising his glass.

The baroness was a *member* of the Society? No wonder she had been sending petulant notes about burrows and cowardice. And so much for the No Females Allowed rule that had stymied them in Munich. Clearly it was a smoke screen to disguise her participation.

But participation to what end?

"I shall tell my housekeeper to prepare a room," the young woman said. "You do not object to the one Her Imperial Majesty so recently vacated? The others, I am afraid, are occupied by Society members."

"We should be honored," Georgia said, offering a smile.

"Gunther, do introduce everyone," the baroness said, rising. "I will return in a moment."

"The Munich papers should be here by now," her husband said, rising also. "Ask the butler to bring them in. Our guests might like to look them over. "

The introductions were performed, and Georgia eyed Fritz Bauer closely, committing his face to memory. Some of them had arrived this morning by train, others by one of the airships at the airfield. How many guest rooms did the castle have if eight or ten or a dozen might arrive, some of them unexpectedly? How were she and Millie to search them all if they were occupied? And most important, what had happened to Mr van Meere and Mr Seacombe? For they must have been on the same train.

She took a deep breath before the questions overwhelmed her. She was, however, certain of two things. One, something significant must have happened to prevent Dustin Seacombe from coming to Marcus's rescue at Burg Salzweg, though she could not imagine what. He was not the sort of man to be prevented by anything if he believed his boy to be in danger. And two, someone had known a lady in waiting was coming and made certain the shells in the game were moved once more.

But the automaton's whereabouts were not important. The whereabouts of the empress were what concerned her.

All right, then. She and Millie were on their own.

No Texicans, no children, no Louise.

A castle of many floors and rooms. And mines. And mountains with innumerable hiding places.

Georgia took a very unladylike gulp of wine.

11:20 a.m.

After discovering that the supply cupboard on pulleys actually did terminate in the kitchens, Cora and Marcus had had a tense couple of minutes earlier, when the scullery maid had opened it and come face to face with people rather than foodstuffs.

Cora had babbled some nonsense about playing a joke on their mother and had scampered through the nearest door before the dumbfounded maid could collect her wits. They had located the staff staircases and begun their search after climbing several dozen sets of stairs. At least, it had seemed like that many. This place being so old, the thick walls behind the rooms in use were riddled with passages and peepholes, which came in very handy.

Cora and Marcus had covered the servants' rooms on both sides of a double-locking door that kept the women from crossing to the men's side and vice versa, but which the two of them working together made short work of. They even searched the attics, which were rather terrifying, especially the one that looked like a bedroom. It had a broken lock on the door that hadn't been touched in probably a century.

Marcus spent ten minutes stifling sneezes after that one.

Now they had reached the family rooms. They were mostly empty of family, though the one that clearly belonged to the baron and his wife had a couple of maids in it, tidying up. Marcus grabbed her hand. *Later*, he mouthed.

Goodness knew there was enough to do on the guest floor. There had to be a dozen rooms, all with doors facing a wide gallery with gloomy pictures hung on the walls. Luckily the staff passage ran along the rear, with plain doors for access and a peephole in each one so you knew whether the guest was awake or absent or standing about with no clothes on. Only one of those was occupied—by a gentleman reading a book in the leather armchair. Fully dressed, thank goodness.

Marcus pulled her along. "None of the other rooms had an automaton in the closet; it's not likely he's got one, either."

The last room must be bigger—they had to jog a little farther along the narrow passage to get to the service door. When Marcus peeped through the hole, he gasped and to Cora's horror, wrenched open the door and practically dove into the room.

Auntie Georgia came out of the water closet just in time to see Marcus fling himself into Auntie Millie's arms. She had been sitting on a luxurious bed with marvelous peacock-blue hangings, so being a lady of a certain age, he rather bowled her over, but she didn't seem to mind.

In fact, she laughed and began to cry at the same time.

"Cora!" Auntie Georgia opened her arms and Cora flew into them. "Oh, my dears, we have been so worried! How has this miracle come about?"

"We've been searching rooms," Cora said. "Since dawn, practically."

"How did you get up here?" Millie had recovered from Marcus's embrace, and blew her nose with the handkerchief tucked into her sleeve. "Surely not in the funicular's carriage —you would have been seen."

"There's a thing like a dumb waiter next to it," Marcus said. "We came up in it to the kitchens. We've searched the attics, the family floor, and all the guest rooms on this floor except for one. It has a gentleman, so we couldn't go in."

"An engineer, no doubt," Georgia said. "There is a meeting

of the Technical Philosophical Society here this afternoon—the people your father and Mr van Meere followed on Friday. A man downstairs—Fritz Bauer—is the last person to have spoken to the empress the day she disappeared. You remember, Cora—the automaton repeated his voice, and we were able to identify him."

"We believe your mother is right, Cora—Bauer kidnapped Christina from her laboratory at Nymphenburg and spirited her somewhere," Millie said. "But where and for what purpose, we do not yet know."

"We have, however, eliminated Hirschfeld from our list of locations," Georgia said with some satisfaction. When both Cora and Marcus must have looked as blank as they felt, she added, "Archduke Rupert's hunting lodge. Millie and I searched it, to no avail, but discovered a tunnel to the river. It was empty."

"From there we escaped on an aquapede," Millie said. "The archduke is probably still wondering what happened to us."

"Brilliant," Marcus said with some admiration. "I have heard of those, but never seen one. But what are you doing here? Where is Pa?"

"And Mama—is she here, too?" Cora asked eagerly.

The animation faded from Auntie Georgia's face. "Not that we know of, darling. But here's a puzzle—I overheard some of the engineers talking downstairs about two members of their party on the train vanishing in the night. Mr Seacombe and Mr van Meere were to have been on the midnight train as well. Something must have happened to make them disembark—something to rival the importance of reaching you, Marcus."

On a map in her mind's eye, Cora traced the route *Thetis*

would have taken from Linderhof to Salzweg, and cross-referenced it with the train route from Munich to Salzburg. "If Mama left Linderhof in *Thetis* to come after us in *Sisi,* she would have flown over the railroad tracks near Chiemsee."

"Nothing would have prevented either of our parents from coming after us," Marcus said flatly. "Nothing except—"

"Remember what I said? She *did* go down in a lake," Cora exclaimed. "There's a train station at Chiemsee for all the holiday-makers. I would wager Bella and Schatzi that your papa and Mr van Meere got off there to help her."

"Don't you dare wager our chickens," Marcus said indignantly. "They're quite safe on *Foresight,* and anyhow, Monsieur LePine wouldn't let you. He likes them."

"It was a figure of speech," she informed him down the length of her nose.

"Figure of speech or no, we do not know for certain that is what happened," Auntie Georgia said. "We must assume we are on our own. How are the two of you going to conceal yourselves? For we are here under false pretenses—Auntie Millie is at present the Margravine von Karlsrühe, and I am posing as her daughter. We haven't any children in our party, and the little ship that brought us here has probably already lifted and gone back to Munich, so we cannot hide you there."

"I had enough hiding aboard *Sisi,*" Marcus said. "We've searched half the house. While you are with the lord and lady and all their company, we'll just keep going."

"This room, for instance," Cora said, looking about her. "It's the last guest room on this floor. Have you searched it?"

"No," Millie admitted. "We had barely walked in when the wall opened and out you popped."

Marcus followed Cora's lead. They had developed a

process for efficiency—look under the bed, in the window seats, water closet, closets. There were two of the latter in this room, big ones for big dresses, Cora supposed. She swung open the doors of the one painted with flowers and birds. Empty, except for a lace cap forgotten on a top shelf.

She looked over at Marcus, doing the same with the other.

"That is my reticule on the shelf, Marcus," Auntie Millie said. "It has food in it, as well as paper and pencil, two moonglobes, and a shawl."

"One never knows," Auntie Georgia said.

"I have nuts in my pockets," Marcus told them. "So does Cora. For the same reason."

Cora was about to close the double doors when something struck her. For such a large wardrobe, it was not very deep. It might manage lace caps and waists, but how could it store the kind of dresses that she'd seen at court, or even the kind Auntie Georgia wore in the evening?

It could only mean one thing.

Leaning in, she examined the rear panels, painted as prettily as the front doors, which was odd in itself. Nobody painted the insides of wardrobes.

"Cora?" Marcus joined her.

"False back," she said absently. "Where's the latch?"

He studied it, too. "What's that?" He touched a bird's eye, painted so realistically it almost twinkled.

Because it's metal, you numpty.

At her indrawn breath, he pressed it and there was a click. The back swung wide, shelves and lace cap and all. And there it was.

"The automaton," Auntie Georgia said in a tone that might as well have been, *Of course it's the automaton.* She sat on the bed with Auntie Millie, her gaze on the motionless form in the shadows of the rear compartment. "That's one piece of this puzzle back in its place."

"Not the one we wanted, but one piece," Auntie Millie allowed.

"The baroness told us the empress returned to Munich this morning," Auntie Georgia said in disgust. "I did not think she would lie to me so soon."

Cora frowned. The baroness's morals were not the point. "So *Sisi* is gone?"

"Yes. I wonder what the crew thought of being sent away when they believed Christina to still be here?"

There was no way to know.

"I do hope we shall not be stranded," Auntie Millie said anxiously. "I wish now we had not refused the offer of *Foresight*."

"Mama will come," Cora assured her. "Even if we are wrong and the gentlemen got off the train for some other reason, Mama will come. She can repair *Thetis*—as long as she has help getting her out of the lake."

Two sets of heavy footsteps passed the door and Auntie Georgia gasped. Silently, Marcus swung the panel back into place and listened for it to latch. Then he closed the wardrobe's doors. "We should get on with the search, Cora."

"What will you do if you are caught?" Auntie Millie asked, not in a worried way, but in a planning sort of way.

When Marcus did not reply, Cora thought fast. The obvious answer made her smile. "We shall say that we are with you. Won't the margravine be surprised when she finds out that her respectable grandchildren have stowed away!"

CHAPTER FIFTEEN

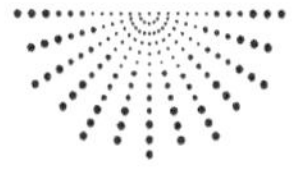

BURG SALZWEG

1:25 p.m.

Cheered immeasurably by the resourcefulness and cleverness of Marcus and Cora, to say nothing of their being alive and well, Georgia tucked Millie's hand in the crook of her elbow and descended to the solar, an affectionate spinster walking her mother down the wide oak staircase. It was best to not know precisely where her supposed niece and nephew were, so that their surprise if they were caught would appear genuine.

But she trusted that they would not be caught.

In the solar, the glasses containing the wine of their welcome had been cleared away, and a pot of tea and two large plates of sandwiches now occupied the sideboard, along with a toothsome looking hazelnut torte on a cake stand and a large tray of petits fours and biscuits. The gentlemen were grazing until it was time for their meeting, and Georgia thought it best that she and Millie should fortify themselves, too.

Since they had left England, all too often one did not know where one's next meal would come from.

Once everyone was safely in the meeting, the two of them could search the main floor, unlikely though it was that someone would keep an empress in the public rooms. The secret passages would likely contain watchful staff members going about their business, too. They must be discreet but thorough.

A plate in one hand and a cup and saucer in the other, she seated herself in an armchair near where Fritz Bauer was perusing the Munich papers, and tucked into her lunch.

He glanced up with a smile.

"Anything of interest, sir?" She took a bite of the next sandwich. Salmon paté. Lovely.

"It seems you have a doppelgänger in the capital, Fraulein. Archduke Rupert attended the Maifest celebrations on the empress's behalf, with a woman very similar to you in appearance upon his arm."

The salmon turned to dust in Georgia's mouth. "Really?" She took a sip of tea and hoped that she had not blushed. "It is said that each of us has a doppelgänger somewhere in the world. I live quietly in Karlsrühe, but I hope she enjoyed dancing with the archduke."

He looked down at the daguerreotype, which appeared to cover the entire top half of the society section. "I did not say she was dancing."

"She must have been, surely? Does the archduke not enjoy it?"

"I'm sure he does—he makes an appearance at every ball and party to which he can cadge an invitation. And with such a beautiful partner, what man would not want to waltz?"

Time to turn the conversation back in his direction. "You do not care for him?"

"I rarely think of him at all." He looked about the room. "Baroness, do come and have a look at the papers. Do you not agree that Fraulein von Karlsrühe bears a striking resemblance to this Lady Langford of whom Archduke Rupert is so enamored?"

Mr Seacombe had used the expression *them's fightin' words* once in Georgia's hearing. Now she understood what he meant.

Baroness Emma Salzmann rustled over, her cheeks flushed and her teeth bared in what Georgia hoped was a smile. "My dear Mr Bauer, please do not insult our guest by comparing her to that hussy."

You are the meek, mild spinster daughter of the margravine. Your only emotion is embarrassment at such language.

Georgia hoped her own high color would be mistaken for a blush of modesty. "Are you acquainted with the lady, ma'am?" she said from behind her teacup.

"Lady! Hardly," the baroness sniffed. She took in the daguerreotype. Of all the times for a newspaper to print a flattering picture! "Hmph. Look at the neckline on that gown. And those jewels—so vulgar. Just like the English to announce their position in society by putting their net worth on their women's necks."

"Is she English?" Bauer scanned the columns of print. "*Ja,* here it is. A widow, staying with Lady Thorne, who is but newly a widow also."

The baroness's contemptuous gaze had not left the picture. She studied it as though she were going to be examined on it later. Then she lifted her lashes to study Georgia in the same manner.

Georgia set down her tea and smiled. "I must see if my mother has everything she needs."

"How curious. You and this Lady Langford have such similar profiles. The arch of the nose is exactly the same. And you are tall, as she is. She can practically look the archduke in the eye."

The jig was up. Georgia knew it in her bones. But she had to play out her part until the end.

"As Mr Bauer said, I must have a doppelgänger. I was not in Munich for Maifest."

"Were not you? It was only yesterday."

"I came to visit my mother, not attend festivals."

"It says here that Lady Thorne has another guest—the aunt of Lady Langford. She would be a woman of a similar age to your mother." Mr Bauer appeared to be following the baroness's train of thought.

"I do not know." Georgia rose. "Please excuse me."

"Not so hasty, Fraulein," the baroness said, her eyes as hard as fired porcelain. "Or should I say Lady Langford? What do you mean by coming here under false pretenses? Oh, do not give me that look of wounded innocence. You are Georgia Brunel and I demand to know what you are doing in my home."

Her tone had caught the attention of the other occupants of the room.

"My dear?" Millie said, rising from her chair. "Is everything all right?"

"And to think I actually curtseyed to you!" The baroness flung out a hand as though to fend off the horrid thought.

"Mama, I think we ought not to inconvenience Lord and Lady Salzmann any longer," Georgia said firmly to Millie, who had drifted nearer, clutching her reticule like a shield in front of her. "I do not understand this, and I fear we are in the way."

"Emma?" The baron set down his plate and crossed the room. "What have you said to make our guests wish to leave us?"

"What have *I* said?" she repeated, her voice rising. "Gunther, we have been imposed upon most dreadfully. This is not the margravine and her daughter. This is Lady Langford, the archduke's latest paramour, and her aunt."

The poor baron was bereft of words.

But his wife was not finished. "Tell us at once—what are you doing here? What do you hope to gain by this flummery?"

Georgia could not make a liar of Millie. She must take responsibility and confess to as much of the truth as she dared. She had just taken a breath when Emma Salzmann leaned in, her eyes snapping with rage.

"He has sent you, hasn't he? He is testing me using the most cruel weapon ever a man devised. To what end? Answer me at once!"

"Emma!" the baron said weakly. "Who are you speaking of? What does this mean?"

Georgia's mind was moving with the speed of a Daimler engine at full throttle. She allowed her gaze to slide to Fritz Bauer. "He ... suspects."

Emma's high color drained away.

I knew it! Fritz Bauer is more than just an engineer. He is—or wants to be—your lover.

"Suspects what?" The baron was coming to himself. "Emma, please explain or I shall become quite cross."

Georgia laid a hand upon his arm. "Your wife has flushed me out, sir, and so I must confess all. It is whispered in Munich that your lady is a member of the Technical Philosophical Society—an organization known to forbid a woman to step over its threshold. There are groups in the universities who are up in arms about it. The Archduke fears a scandal, so he has sent me to find out the truth before the empress herself is dragged into it."

"Of course my wife is a member," the baron protested. "But why should there be a scandal?"

"Because I am the only woman allowed over said threshold," Emma said. Clever girl, going along with such a tale. "There are female engineering students now—even women in development positions at the Zeppelin Airship Works. It is clear that Mr Bauer and his colleagues must either go public and allow women to be members, or quash the rumors and keep my membership a secret."

"But you are brilliant," he protested. "What of the papers you have written? How will they be published if you are not a member?"

"I am quite content to do my work behind the scenes, my dear," she told him. Georgia could hear the sincerity in her voice. She would give anything to know what kind of work she really meant—and how it involved the substitution of the automaton for the empress.

"I am to return to Munich when I have something to report," she said now to Emma. "What may I tell the archduke?"

The baroness bit back something she clearly wanted to say

very badly. "You may tell him the rumors are completely untrue, and that the baron and I remain his loyal friends, in quiet retirement here at Salzweg."

Oh, how those words cost her! Georgia had no doubt she would exact a price for her having made her say them, too.

"We will go now, if you will be so kind as to allow us the use of your chauffeur and landau?"

"Certainly." Emma rang the bell.

"But—but surely not," the baron said. "You were to have stayed for dinner. And what about—"

His wife laid a hand on his arm, and tucked her curvy self up against him. "We must not detain the archduke's emissaries, Gunther. Everything is out in the open now."

Georgia thanked him for his hospitality, and collected Millie, who looked close to combustion, she had so many questions.

"Allow me to see you to the carriage," Emma said, leaving her husband and rustling into the grand entry with them. "No, no, not that way. I am sure you do not wish to advertise your comings and goings. Servants do talk, and they all know you were to have stayed the night. This corridor is more discreet."

She opened a door concealed behind a tapestry and beckoned them to follow her. As soon as the door closed, she set off at a brisk pace.

"Now that we are alone, perhaps you will tell me why you are really here, Lady Langford. For it is not because of my membership in the Society."

"Certainly not. Though something makes me wish women were indeed welcome in those hallowed halls."

Emma laughed, a tinkling sound as empty as a spoon

inside a teacup. "Most women would not have the stomach for what the Society really does. Half the male members do not, either. That is why a woman with a firm hand and a quick mind is necessary."

They followed her down a set of stone steps, though Georgia could have sworn the solar had been on the same level as the courtyard.

"And what does the Society really do?" Millie asked from the rear. "Read monographs about other people's inventions and replicate them?"

"You *are* well informed." Emma's tone mocked her. "No, we have bigger fish to fry, chief among them being the establishment on the throne of someone who is more capable of running the empire than a misplaced engineer or a buffoon."

"Someone such as yourself?" Georgia asked, hoping she sounded innocent.

Emma snorted. "No, indeed. But my son will have royal blood, and once I marry Rupert, will be brought up with a far more pertinent education than either Christina or Rupert received. He will be a new Caesar, and the empire will enter its golden age."

The woman was stark, staring mad. "Is that why you and the Society kidnapped the empress, and substituted her automaton?"

A glance over her shoulder betrayed the woman's surprise. But she did not answer, merely opened another door and indicated they should enter a large, very old room that might have been one of the original chapels. Now it held only a lumpy bed, a chair, and a table on which were spread newspapers similar to the ones that had betrayed Georgia upstairs.

"Can we board the carriage from here?" Millie asked.

"No. But I will tell my husband that you did. If you are so clever, perhaps you can find the empress yourselves." She shrugged. "She was here, but I see that she is not now. Since there is no way out but the way we came in, and that door there—" She nodded across the room. "She will not have got far."

"What do you plan to do with her?" Georgia asked, moving casually to her right. She must not let their hostess reach the door.

Emma glanced back. "Why, nothing. Or with you, either. But an announcement will be made that she has abdicated her throne in favor of a private life of invention and scholarship. She will never be heard from again, and her reign will simply be a brief prologue to the most glorious epoch the empire has ever known."

With a curse at her own foolishness in allowing herself to be led down here, Georgia leaped, but the baroness was too quick for her. She whipped behind the very thick medieval door and slammed it, and a heavy lock turned.

"Good-bye, Lady Langford," came a muffled voice. "I will comfort the archduke as best I can when he learns you were called suddenly back to England."

Georgia banged on the door with both fists, but got nothing for her pains but … pain.

She controlled herself, only to find Millie had turned her back on her. And no wonder. How stupid she must think her, walking so meekly into this trap and not using her brain at all! And now Millie was probably going to starve to death along with her and it was all Georgia's fault.

"Millie—I'm such a fool—"

"No, you're not."

"I should have known what she was doing the moment she held up that tapestry. We are going to die down here, and neither of us will—" *See Mr Seacombe or Mr van Meere again.*

"Georgia, look. Under the bed."

Millie bent by the bed, and Georgia joined her. *Oh, please don't let there be rodents.*

There weren't. A young woman in her early twenties lay under it as though hiding, her eyes huge in a face that was pale and sick. A face Georgia knew.

Without thought or volition, her knees bent in a curtsey. "Your Imperial Majesty," she breathed in horror.

"I was," the girl whispered. "Who the devil are you?"

CHAPTER SIXTEEN

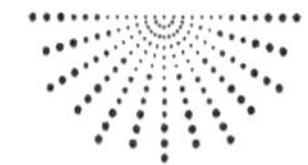

BURG SALZWEG

*C*ora and Marcus held their breaths, crammed in as far as they could go under the ancient oak staircase, peeking through cracks in the risers as the blond lady hurried past. Cora had heard her lock the door behind the tapestry, and while half of her hoped to see Auntie Georgia and Auntie Millie hurry out with her, the more pessimistic half was not surprised when they did not.

The lady had locked them into whatever lay beyond that door.

She went directly to the solar and closed the door behind her, whereupon people's voices rose. Cora let out her breath.

"Let's go," Marcus whispered. "Do you have a good nut?"

She pulled a Brazil nut out of her pocket and showed him. After making sure the coast was clear, they ran across the grand entry hall, pulled up the tapestry, and unlocked the door. They slipped inside and, just in case someone should think to lock the door and trap them in there, too, slid the nut into the lock housing. It was still in its shell, and since Cora had never succeeded in shelling a Brazil nut without a hammer, the chances of its working might be good.

It was nearly dark in the corridor, except for some very poor electricks running along near the ceiling. There were also a lot more closed doors.

"How are we going to find them?"

"Try all the doors?"

"I'll leave a peanut by all the ones we try, so we don't get mixed up."

"The rats will be happy. All right, then. Let's go find out what she did with Auntie Georgia and Auntie Millie." Somewhere along the line, Marcus had adopted Cora's informal form of address. "The only way out is forward."

This philosophy had served them well in Venice. Down the corridor they went, trying doors, checking to see if there were people, finding storage rooms and hallways that angled off to other places.

"Lots of hiding spots, at any rate," Marcus whispered. That was in their favor. The blond lady did not look like the sort of woman who would be happy to find two strange children hiding in the staff passages.

Cora was running out of peanuts by the time the passage stopped being a corridor and turned into an old tunnel. She didn't want the rats to have the hazelnuts, or the almonds, either, so it was a relief to stop at a particularly heavy door that blocked the way, and which looked to be as old as the staircase. Maybe even made from the same tree.

Marcus knelt to examine the lock. "No key. She must have taken it with her."

Cora felt rather smug. "Who needs keys when you have hairpins?"

She wasn't quite so smug ten minutes later, when the lock refused to cooperate. Another ten minutes, and she was beginning to perspire. "I need a second tool. Something straight, that I can press with."

"Back in a minute."

It was a lot longer than a minute by the time Marcus ran into view. "Sorry," he panted. "Maids." He held up a long, thin bit of metal about the length of his forefinger.

"What's this?"

"Dunno, but the engine they were using to heat their irons stopped working when I pulled it out."

She wanted to giggle, but lock-picking was serious work. Cora set to her task again, feeling the innards of the lock—getting reacquainted with it—gently persuading it. And with a click, it yielded.

Marcus hauled her up—her legs had gone to sleep—and waited for her to shake the pins and needles out before he opened the door. Cora secured the metal part in her hair with the hairpin in case they needed it again, and followed him in.

Auntie Georgia whirled, her eyes wide with panic. Her jaw dropped for a moment before she recovered herself, and she fell to her knees to hug them as they ran into her arms. "You blessed children, what wonders you are!"

"We were watching from under the stairs and saw that lady take you through the door under the tapestry," Cora said. "We tried every door all along here, but this was the worst one. The lock didn't want to open."

"I'm very glad it did." She got to her feet. "The empress is very ill. We need to get her somewhere safe as soon as possible."

The empress?

"You're sure she's not an automaton?" Marcus sounded skeptical as he regarded the poor creature lying in the bed. "She doesn't look a bit like the lady on the stamps."

"*She* is the cat's grandmother," the girl rasped.

Marcus looked startled. "I beg your pardon, Ma'am."

"We've been feeding her what bits of food we have in hopes she might regain some strength," Millie said, tipping a blue glass bottle of water to the girl's lips.

She drank obediently.

"Not too much," Marcus said. "A little at a time. Otherwise she'll be sick."

"How do you know?" Cora demanded. "She's thirsty."

"I live in a desert. Auntie Millie, we have nuts, too."

"Best save them for later," Auntie Georgia said grimly. "While we look after Her Imperial—"

"Christina," the girl said, her voice a little stronger. "This is no time for titles."

"Quite so," Auntie Georgia agreed. "You two might explore what's behind that door there." She nodded to the far side of the cavelike chamber, carved out of the rock. "Baroness Salzmann said we might go out that way, which tells me it is a hopeless case. But I should like to know, all the same."

"We can always go back out the door behind the tapestry. We put a Brazil nut in the lock." But clearly a question for the empress was burning on Marcus's lips. "How long have you been down here, Ma'am?"

"No idea," Christina said. "One minute I was in my laboratory, the next I was here. First they gagged me, then chloroformed me."

Cora made a face. Horrible, nasty stuff. Mama had used it

for something in her laboratory and had come close to swooning.

"That was last Sunday," Auntie Millie said. "You've been here a week, and your automaton has been performing your duties in your place."

Her dull eyes brightened. "And no one realized it?"

Millie shook her head. "No one but Louise Thorne." She tilted her silvery head at Cora. "Cora's mother, who was on her way down here and has not yet arrived."

"That's because she might have gone down in Chiemsee," Cora said. "She'll be along. Have they not been feeding you, Ma'am?"

"There was food at first, while they decided what they were doing." Christina breathed deeply, as though gathering strength for speech. "They must have made up their minds, for I've had nothing for three days. More water, please."

"I had the distinct impression we were all to be skeletons when we were finally found, a century from now," Auntie Georgia said grimly, watching the water go down. "Cora and Marcus, off you go. I want to know what's through there, and I do not wish to leave Christina."

The door opened easily—though it was another heavy one. "Not a good sign," Marcus muttered. "Get the prisoner's hopes up and dash them at the end? That's just mean. Here's another tunnel."

"It's noisy," Cora said. "Like machinery. We came down a couple of staircases back there. Is this the way into a mine?"

In a moment, their questions were answered. The tunnel widened out to a kind of open stone balcony, where the brightness of the sky stabbed Cora's eyes. Was it still only afternoon outside, far away from stuffy corridors and nasty plots to kill people?

She squinted through her lashes until her eyes adjusted. Then she and Marcus cautiously investigated the lip of the rock shelf.

"Oh, my." She stumbled back and fetched up against a stone face. "It must be a mile straight down."

Marcus stood back from the edge a judicious couple of boot lengths, and craned to look over. "Not quite. A thousand feet, maybe."

"That's nine hundred and ninety-seven feet too many."

Leaning on this rock face, she could see for a mile, though. Nothing but mountainsides and granite thrusting up into the sky, and scraggly pine trees and snow.

She shuddered and studied the shelf closer to home. A pile of bones lay just beyond where she stood, where the ledge narrowed to only three or four feet. She devoutly hoped they were not human, but she was not about to edge closer to investigate.

"It's cold." She buttoned her cardigan closed.

"There's a mine mouth just here," Marcus reported, looking to the left. "It must be one of the oldest ones, right under the house. The carts aren't very full, though. Maybe it's playing out."

She screwed up her courage and sidled next to him, leaning out just enough to see the carts come out of the mine mouth, attached to hooks on the funicular, and go over the drop in a sickening fashion, yet without tipping and dumping their valuable loads. The funicular stopped at another mouth, then another about three hundred feet from the bottom. At each stop, it collected carts. The entire business seemed to operate by itself—unless the operators were standing just inside, out of the weather.

"This is why that lady told Auntie Georgia they could go out the door," Marcus said in disgust. "All the illusion of freedom they could want. Until they starved to death looking at it."

Cora resisted the urge to glance at the bones. "She's cruel, that lady." She couldn't stand it anymore—not the cold, and not the indifferent mountains. "Come on. Let's report back."

3:25 p.m.

Thank heaven the food seemed to be reviving Christina. By the time the children returned, she had finished the bottle of water and eaten the second apple and another wedge of the cheese from Millie's reticule. Georgia thought they had better save the children's nuts for later, when the empress's strength gave out. She must have a strong constitution, for she was able now to swing her booted feet to the floor and pay close attention to the children's report.

"The funiculars are not manned, except from the bottom," she said in response to Marcus's speculations. "The Salzmann family have had two centuries to perfect the system. Some of them—the *Heimbergswerk*, the home works—have been operating nearly that long. Tell me, in which direction are we facing?"

Cora made a face. "I don't know. Toward a lot of mountains and more mines. If you can walk a little ways, you can see for yourself."

Georgia started to demur, but Christina was already on her feet. "It is all right, Georgia. I am coming back to myself.

Hope seems to have the same effect on the mind as water and food do on the body."

Still, she took Georgia's arm as they all walked the short distance down the tunnel. Marcus showed her the funicular coming out of the mine mouth, while Cora indicated the pile of bones.

Christina frowned. "I sincerely hope that is not one of the baron's wives."

Millie gasped. "What do you mean, Ma'am?"

"The first died of an infectious fever bearing a stillborn child. The second suffered a climbing accident a couple of years ago—or so the papers said. The area where she fell is so remote they could not recover the body. Not long afterward, the baron married again, poor man. To that harpy who fancies herself the future Regent."

"She told you her plan, did she?" Georgia stepped gingerly back from the brink and focused her attention on the funicular on the left, fervently hoping her stomach would stop swooping like a bird in flight.

"She did, clearly believing I would take the secret to the grave she has made of that room. Which I would have, had it not been for you and the children." She smiled at them, her face blossoming into an approximation of the beauty that privation had stolen from her.

But Georgia's attention was caught on a possibility. "Christina, would you say this ledge is wide enough to reach that funicular?"

The empress followed her gaze. "No."

"Oh, come. It narrows, but is still a good twelve inches wide before the gap to the channel in which the cogs move."

"And what sights do you plan to take in from there before you plunge to your death?"

"I plan to take myself into one of those carts and make my way to the base of the mountain."

"Topping!" Marcus dashed toward the narrow part of the ledge.

Christina grabbed the collar of his shirt as he passed and nearly lost her footing. "Not so fast, my lad. Even if you could ride all the way to the bottom, you'd still have a walk of at least a day to get round to the side where the town is. And while I'm upright at present, I cannot guarantee I will be able to keep up."

"Then what about those mine mouths we can see?" Millie pointed at them—one, two, three. "Have you been inside? Would any of them take us through to the south?"

"I say," the empress said with some admiration, "you do have gumption. It has been some time since I was first given a tour, but if I recall, the middle one may do so. But I must caution you that—"

A boom like a clap of thunder came from down the tunnel, and far off, a woman screeched in rage.

"It's her!" Cora gasped. "The Brazil nut failed!"

"Quick, into the carts! Marcus and Cora, you first." Georgia pushed them both ahead of her and they scampered along the ledge like mountain goats. Marcus waited for a cart to descend and then leaped into it. Cora jumped into the next one.

Baroness Salzmann was far enough along the tunnel now that they could make out words. "What have they done with her? Fritz!"

Christina launched herself along the ledge as though she

had been prodded with a sword, and scrambled into a cart, which swung in a sickening fashion as it took her down the precipice.

"Millie, we have no choice. Take my hand."

Though Millie's lips were tightly pressed together, Georgia could still hear her keening with fear as they edged along the ledge. But there was no time for fear. A cart descended past their heads, and when it was low enough to see inside—half full, thank goodness—Georgia put an arm around her waist and launched them both into it.

They landed on a hard and very knobbly heap of purple salt crystals the size of her fists.

"Duck!"

The next iron cart swung above their heads, giving at least a little cover from the hunters above.

"How do we get out?" Millie gasped.

"The same way we got in. We must watch what the others do. I believe it slows while new carts are added."

She could hear indistinct voices from above, all but the sound of rage carried away on the wind. She didn't suppose the baroness would think they'd all leaped to their deaths in despair. She was too cunning for that. The first place she would look was down the funicular. Their only chance was to get into the mine mouth before they were spotted.

The cogs clanked as their speed slowed. "Get ready, dearest."

And here was Marcus, leaning in to take Millie's hand. "Hurry, Auntie. They've seen us."

Georgia scrambled out after her, flinging a panicked glance over her shoulder. Seventy feet above, she had a foreshortened view of the baroness's teeth bared in a snarl as her hair blew around her face.

Holding hands, she and Millie ran into the mine. It was like running into the pit of hell, their ears assaulted by the clank and crash of the carts as they came up on their cogs, their noses by the smell of winding grease and hot metal and the ferric scent of carts and rock.

"Here!" Marcus shouted, and vanished into the pit. Cora leaped in after him, feet first.

Georgia shrieked, though no one could hear her in all the racket. Christina yanked on Millie's hand and the three of them pitched over the edge—

—onto a slide of polished wood.

Now Millie screamed as they slid down the precipitous incline and wound up with a thump and a roll at the bottom.

"You're supposed to go feet first," Christina said, hauling Georgia upright while Marcus helped Millie.

"I think I broke something," Millie said sadly, opening her reticule and pulling out a shard of a moonglobe. The liquid within dripped on the rock floor.

"Never mind. Come on," Christina urged them. "There are more descents. But we may simply find our pursuers have taken the sensible course and gone down to meet us in the passenger carriage."

"Is there a way to get to the airfield?" Cora asked as they loped down the sloping tunnel. "Auntie Georgia is good at stealing airships."

"Cora, must you confess my sins to the empress?" Georgia moaned. "She is likely Colonel in Chief of the army and is thus empowered to make arrests."

"I shan't arrest you," Christina assured her. "If we get out of this, I'm more likely to give you a medal. All of you."

"We may not steal a ship, but we might hide in one and send a pigeon to *Sisi*." Millie seemed to be recovering from being sent down a chute like a load of laundry.

"Or *Thetis*," Cora said.

"Or *Foresight*," Marcus suggested. "Here we are. Aunties, try to go down feet first this time."

Georgia tried, but it was not easy. The bottom was invisible in the insufficient light of the electricks, so there was no way to prepare oneself for the landing. Was this really how the miners got from one level to the other? There were no stairs, so how did—

A man's voice hailed them from the funicular, leaning out of a cart and gaping in astonishment at the sight of three women and two children whooshing down the chute. He vanished upward in the gloom.

"Bother," Cora said. "He will tell on us."

And then they landed, and they could do nothing but pick themselves up and run to the next one. And the next. At the bottom, Christina could barely push herself to her feet. "I feel—"

Silently, she crumpled to the ground.

"Christina!" Georgia knelt beside her, pressing her fingers to her pulse. Steady. Thank goodness for that. "Millie, is there any more water?"

"No, she's had it all."

"I have an apple," Marcus said, producing it, slightly squashed, from his pocket. "Well, most of it."

"The squashed bit," Georgia said. "Put it in her mouth. Perhaps there will be enough moisture and sweetness to help."

She sent up a prayer of thanks when Christina recovered enough to suck the pulp, and in moments was finishing off the apple and a handful of almonds besides. Marcus distributed chunks of cheese—only slightly the worse for wear from pockets and slide—and cut the remaining apple in quarters with his pocketknife.

Though Georgia had had lunch, it seemed like a week ago. After even such scant provisions as these, she felt almost ready to tackle another wretched slide.

"Christina, can you remember a way to the airfield?" She had not been able to answer before she fainted. "One that won't attract attention?"

"Only the river," the empress said slowly. "But I am afraid I cannot swim."

"It's not that deep a river," Marcus said. "I looked from the bridge. There were fish. And lots of stones away at the bottom."

"But there are boats and barges to squash us and run us over," Cora objected. "We'd better risk the road."

A risky plan was better than none.

Georgia helped the empress to her feet and, with Millie on her other side, they set off again, this time heading toward the dim glow of the mine mouth in the distance—and the golden light of late afternoon.

CHAPTER SEVENTEEN

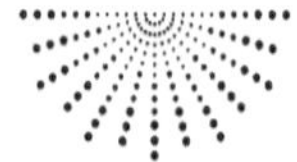

*I*f there was one thing Dustin Seacombe hated, it was not being able to act decisively to solve a problem.

He stood at the starboard viewing port in *Thetis*'s gondola, glaring at the mountains that rose all around them as they neared the town of Salzweg. In the distance, he could just make out the pinnacle on which the castle stood, the latter seeming to be an extension growing out of the former.

"I wish I knew exactly where they were," he growled. "How is this going to go if they haven't found the children?"

"Consider rather that Cora will find Georgia and Millie," Louise told him from the navigation table. "They will all be together by now, you may be sure of it."

Once *Thetis* had been repaired and was fully flightworthy, Louise had reluctantly surrendered the helm to Cornelius. Dustin's employer was in such a state of apprehension and grim determination that it gave him something to do besides stumping around the little airship and throwing it off trim.

"Cornelius, half a point to port and we will see the airfield in two minutes," she said, glancing between land forms and maps. "As for our friends, you and Dustin are known to the Technical Philosophical Society, and one of you to the Salzmanns by reputation. You will have easy entrance to the castle while I conduct my own search."

Since Louise was known to the baroness, and known to be a confidante of the empress, it made sense that she should stay out of sight. Instead, she would enter through the *Heimsalzbergwerk.* "The baroness and I were thrown together occasionally at Nymphenburg, and there being nothing of note to say about Kastanienhof, she was happy to tell me about her husband's property. The home mine, apparently, was dug before the castle was built upon its profits. There are entrances that will take me into the cellars of the house."

From above, the airfield looked to be of the informal kind, with more emphasis on *field* than *air*. Three airships were moored below, and there was not even the usual office where flight plans might be filed. Just a lot of what looked like apple trees.

"Where is *Sisi?*" Louise demanded as Cornelius banked into a circle, having decided upon his moorage. "Has the automaton been moved again? For they cannot have known I was coming. Bother it! If Cora and Marcus have gone with her—"

"They would not, if Miss Brunel and Lady Langford were at the castle." Dustin laid a hand in brief consolation on her shoulder. "They would have sent a pigeon. Regardless of the automaton's whereabouts, I think we can still assume all four are here."

He could only hope he was right.

Over Louise's shoulder, sudden motion in the narrow valley caught his eye. "What's this? Bring her around again."

Though halfway through their approach, Louise obligingly told the automaton intelligence system to take them up.

With this unobstructed view, Dustin leaned into the forward viewing port. Four slender figures—no, five—were making their way up the road, two of them assisting the fifth, who was clearly in distress. And in the distance behind them, a company of men in uniform were marching in a phalanx, their smart pace telling Dustin they were out for more than routine exercises.

On the road— "Those are our friends!" he exclaimed. "And if that's not the empress herself, you can call me a fool and let me ride facing the horse's a—"

Louise sucked in a breath. "Go astern and let down the basket before they're apprehended!"

He ran as fast as his boots could carry him down the short corridor, past the engine room and the communications cage, and opened the hatch leading to the external vanes and propellers at the stern. The winch that operated the basket was connected by piping to the Daimlers, so all he had to do was push up the lever that allowed steam pressure to propel its engine.

The basket spooled downward on its rope as Cornelius brought the nimble little ship around in a tight corkscrew.

Their friends had seen them now. The children raced on ahead to grab the basket and hold it steady.

"Hurry!" Dustin urged them, one eye on the blessed sight

of his boy, well and unharmed, the other on the guards, whose company had divided and was coming on fast in a pincer formation.

Once they all got their hands on the basket, the jig was up.

Georgia and Millie were half carrying the empress now. What had the poor woman been through that she was all but unable to save herself? Ten steps—five—

The commander of the guards shouted an order and they moved in to seize their prey.

The two women gave a mighty heave and flung the empress into the basket. Georgia boosted Millie in.

"You're out of time!" Dustin hollered, to no effect whatsoever, since he was fifty feet in the air, his voice drowned out by wind and engines. But Cora and Marcus could calculate a short approach as well as anyone—they abandoned their posts and scrambled up the basket's sides. That left Georgia in the gate, on her stomach, legs kicking, with Millie tugging her in by both arms.

She wasn't all the way in, but he had no choice. He slammed the reverse lever over and the basket rose—a second too late.

One of the guards dropped his rifle, jumped, and grabbed two handfuls of skirt. The basket tilted and Georgia screamed as Millie heroically braced herself with both feet on either side of the gate and hung on to her arm. Georgia kicked out violently and her flight boot caught the guard on the chin, sending him over backward. The basket swung in the other direction. But it rose unimpeded, swinging like a pendulum, the wicker gate flapping back and forth uselessly as Millie, Marcus, and Cora hauled with all their strength on whatever part of Georgia's anatomy they could grab.

Dustin's lungs lost their ability to work until she got a knee under her and could crawl in under her own steam, lying flat in the bottom with both hands gripping the sturdy weave as though she would never let go.

The basket had not even docked before Cornelius took *Thetis* up, well out of range of the guards' old-fashioned rifles. What were they thinking, attempting to shoot at their anointed monarch?

But of course a dead empress would only allow the baroness and the Society to put their plans in motion sooner rather than later.

"Dad!" Marcus leaped out and flung himself into Dustin's arms. "That was close!"

He breathed in his son's scent—sweat and dirt and cotton. "Too close," he said into the boy's shoulder. "Nice work. Now, take Cora to her mother. I'll see to the ladies."

The empress and Millie came off first, each as white and shaking as the other. "Welcome aboard, Your Imperial Majesty." Then he said to Millie, "Take her to the first cabin on the left, ma'am. If you can get her there, we'll see you both tended to."

"I'm all right," Millie said on a gasp. The empress was weeping with exhaustion and pain, as Millie supported her through the hatch. "Only a little farther, my dear. You've been very brave. Just a few more steps."

Dustin turned in time to see Georgia stagger to her feet, bracing herself with her hands on the gate as she got it closed at last. He reached out to secure her, and to his surprise, she allowed it. And then, his body slipped the sensible reins of his brain.

He pulled her into his arms and simply held her while she

wept as noisily as a child, the wind pulling at their clothes, the scent of winding grease and canvas in their nostrils as little *Thetis* fell up into the safety of the sky.

And Dustin knew beyond all doubt that he did not wish to be parted from this brave, beautiful, irreplaceable woman ever again.

Friday, May 24, 1895
Aboard Sisi, 1:40 p.m.

"It is Queen Victoria's birthday," Millie said, apropos of nothing

They were waiting in her private royal saloon for Empress Christina's arrival. *Sisi* was moored in the royal airfield in the great park behind Nymphenburg Palace.

"How I wish I were home to celebrate—the village with its bunting and flags, the ball at Langford Park." She sighed.

Outside *Sisi*'s viewing port, one or two of the household airships bobbed gently at their moorings, along with another of the Zeppelin LZ-48 airships that Georgia had toured. It could not be the same one, but she had no doubt to whom it belonged—Archduke Rupert. She and Millie had already concluded he must have been summoned to the palace for a royal dressing-down. And possibly even to be disinherited in favor of some distant relative less likely to tangle themselves in treason.

"Are you homesick, dearest?" Georgia asked gently. "I confess that I shall be glad to see the woods and fields of Langford again. It is always so lovely in May."

"Not homesick … exactly," Millie mused. "Though if you

wish to go home, I should not object. A brief period of rest with no excitement whatsoever would be most welcome."

"The lakes of northern Italy?" Georgia said idly, picking up her cup and saucer. "The south of France?"

"Somewhere restful, dull, and warm," Millie agreed. "While we could likely find the first two anywhere in England, the third does mean the Continent, I'm afraid."

Outside, the singing of an approaching landau was nearly drowned out by the raucous clatter of a small engine, which abruptly ceased. *Sisi* bobbed in a curtsey, signifying that the royal party was coming aboard.

Detaching themselves from the chattering ladies in waiting, Marcus and Cora ran into the saloon, Louise Thorne at their heels. "Hallo, Aunties," Cora said, collecting kisses from them both. "Have you left us any tea?"

"There are masses of cakes and tarts and gallons of tea," Georgia assured her.

The children ran over to the buffet to investigate, while Mr Seacombe and Mr van Meere came in more quietly with Empress Christina and Landgräfin Winter. The former was dressed in loden green bloomers trimmed with scallops of black velvet on the cuffs, and an intricately cut waist of Brussels lace with a high collar that suited her upswept hair.

"Goodness me, enough of that," the empress said, waving them out of their curtsies. "I'm famished after the day I've had. Come, Landgräfin, ladies, gentlemen—let us eat everything in sight."

Several days of feeding up and healthy draughts prepared by the court physicians had brought the empress's energy back, and her face was filling out again. As she led the way to the buffet, Georgia caught Dustin Seacombe's eye. His crinkled in a smile under the brim of that disreputable hat, while she blushed at the memory of her own behavior at the stern of *Thetis*, alone on the windy platform. She had had every excuse in the world to go to pieces in his arms—near death, near capture—but still. She had believed herself to be made of sterner stuff.

Perhaps sterner stuff had to be built up, like one's muscles when learning to ride.

When they all had a plate of food and were seated in an arrangement of chairs and sofas that facilitated conversation, Christina said, "I know you are all interested to know the details of my activities these last few days. You may speak freely in front of Landgräfin Winter—I know she assisted you in this affair."

"Did your men find the automaton where we said it would be?" Marcus asked eagerly. "In the painted wardrobe at the castle?" His father nudged him. "Ma'am?"

"Yes, my dear, they did, thank you very much." Her smile faded. "Your father advises me to destroy it, lest someone get the bright idea to try this again."

"Destroy the automaton!" Louise exclaimed. "After all that work? Oh, surely not."

"It's a beautiful piece," Georgia agreed. "It seems a shame. But Mr Seacombe is right. If the Technical Philosophical Society can kidnap you and substitute the thing so easily, it won't be long before someone else does, too."

"And no telling if you'll have friends about you to help," the Landgräfin added.

Mr van Meere looked up. "What about this museum the Association of German Engineers is talking about building on that big island in the Isar? They want to name it something unwieldy like the German Museum of Masterpieces of Science and Technology. Typical. But if they ever get it built, your automaton would certainly qualify."

Christina tilted her head as she considered the idea. "That would be less distressing than taking a sledgehammer to my plaything. I shall have to find a place to store it until it's wanted, where it can't be found."

Marcus and Cora looked at one another. "Linderhof," they said simultaneously, and both Louise and Christina laughed.

"So your men were at Burg Salzweg?" Georgia asked cautiously. "Did they find the Society members still there?"

"No. They scarpered the moment they realized their secret was exposed. But we will find them, never fear." The lines of her young face settled into grim angles. "The Salzmanns are under house arrest, with guards at every door and mine entrance. I must make some decisions about the baroness."

"Clap her in gaol," Mr Seacombe growled.

"I would, except for the baby," Christina said. "My ministers advise me to leave her under house arrest until the child is delivered, and then have her executed for treason."

Marcus swallowed his bite of fruit tart audibly. Georgia narrowly missed doing the same.

"Until then, I am certain her torment will be acute, since the baron has been fully apprised of his wife's perfidy."

"And what of the archduke?" Millie ventured. "He was rather, er, intimately involved, was he not?"

"It is too early to tell." Christina glanced at the children.

"Oh, you can talk in front of us," Cora assured her. "Believe me, I have heard worse things in my missions as a spy."

"I am sure you have." Christina chucked her under the chin

with a finger. "Very well. Apparently there are not two, but three possible fathers for the child."

Good heavens. The poor baron, to endure such knowledge after so much hope. "Fritz Bauer," Georgia said with certainty. "I knew it."

"So he admits, being still at the castle when my men arrived. The baron, of course, may choose to acknowledge the child as his, especially if it is the long-awaited male heir. Rupert cannot acknowledge it at all to polite society, and Herr Bauer—" She waved a hand. "Fatherhood or the lack thereof will not matter to him in gaol. Rupert does not deny the affair, but he certainly denies any intent to marry the widow once she had done away with her husband. He assures me of his constant loyalty."

"I'm sure he does," Georgia said with a sniff. "I suppose *he*, at least, is in no danger of being executed for treason. Did he know of the Empress Regent plot?"

With a roll of her eyes, Christina said, "He says not, the silly fool. Honestly, if there was a single other candidate to inherit the throne, I should choose them instantly."

"You shall simply have to marry to solve the problem," Millie told her. "What about that handsome Danish prince? Or one of Queen Victoria's grandsons?"

"*Et tu, Brute?*" Christina complained. "You and my ministers are all singing from the same choir book."

Millie looked stricken, lest she had been too forward, until the empress twinkled at her.

"Never mind, Millie. I have no patience for princes—goodness knows I've been paraded in front of enough of them. I shall marry a decent, hardworking scientist, like your good queen, and simply elevate him to the nobility. Problem solved."

Georgia applauded. "Well said, Ma'am. So Herr Bauer's fate is decided? Was he the ringleader?"

"To some extent. I do not believe he was privy to the Empress Regent plot, as he had fond hopes of the widow consoling herself with him. Still, his was the brain that conceived of the automaton's part in my kidnapping, so he must feel the consequences."

"And you are safe?" Mr van Meere asked, gazing at her over a teacup that seemed tiny in his big hands. "No miscreants yet lurking in the salt mines?"

"I believe not." She set her empty plate aside, slapped her hands on her knees, and rose. "Come—let us think of happier things. It is a beautiful day and I have something to show you all."

How wonderful to know that Christina could now act on her own royal behalf and consign her enemies to her courts of law. What a weight it must have lifted from those slender shoulders. A walk outside seemed just the thing.

They strolled down *Sisi*'s gangway while Cora explained how she and Marcus had boarded the ship through the communications cage.

Christina laughed. "You two are endlessly inventive. What a pity you cannot attend the *Kindertechnik* here and put your skills to good use. Once the Lycée des Jeunes Filles gets hold of you, there is no escape. Ah, here we are. Let us go round to the LZ-48's stern. I want to see if you can board her the same way."

Georgia was not sure the archduke would like his new airship treated so cavalierly, but people in disgrace ought not to be particular. Besides, the royal ships might belong to the government in any case.

Marcus boosted Cora up, and the girl scrambled into the chute. "I'm in," she called, and a few seconds after Marcus's boots, too, disappeared, they heard, "So am I."

Christina leaned in as though the chute were a speaking horn. "Go forward, then, and let down the gangway. The automaton intelligence system does not yet know its owner's voice."

It didn't take long to walk the length of the fuselage to the gangway. Once inside, Georgia looked about her as the empress led them into the saloon. "It's just as lovely as the one I toured at the airship works," she sighed. "Oh, to own a vessel like this!"

"I'm glad you like it, Georgia," the empress said cheerfully. "Because it's registered in your name and Millie's both."

She heard the words, but they made no sense.

Cora shrieked and flung her arms about her. "Auntie Georgia, you're so lucky!"

"I—I—what?" she said feebly, sitting rather suddenly on a sofa upholstered in a delicious pattern of daffodils. "Isn't this the archduke's ship?"

"It was. My government confiscated it. That will teach him to choose his friends better." Christina looked enormously pleased with herself. "And now I've made it over to you. For services rendered to the Crown."

"Oh, Ma'am." Tears swam in her eyes. She took Millie's hand as though it might anchor her reeling mind. "We couldn't possibly. It's far too—"

"It's not nearly enough," Christina interrupted her. "Rupert is in disgrace. My ministers are still in the dark. The three of you, on the other hand, took on the solving of my disappearance in true Holmesian style, at risk of life and limb. Yes, Louise told me you have read everything Sir Arthur has written."

Louise looked rather smug.

"As for you, my dear friend," the empress said to her, "when Parliament opens again in the autumn, I shall create you Margravine von Kastaniensee, and the house, the lake, and all five thousand acres of producing land shall be deeded to you and your heirs in perpetuity."

Louise gaped at her. "But—but we are only renting it. How—"

"It is a crown holding," Christina said. "In my gift. For services rendered."

Georgia would not have believed Louise Thorne capable of tears had she not witnessed them sliding down her cheeks.

"So we do not have to go back to England, Ma'am?" Cora asked, her eyes wide. "We can stay here, and you and Mama can still be friends?"

Christina cupped the child's face with both hands, and kissed her nose. "If Mama agrees, I think that is a lovely plan. And should the time come when you must return, you may sell the place and live many years on the proceeds."

"I hope we don't sell it," Cora said. "I love Kastanienhof. And I love you." She threw her arms around the monarch, who hugged her tightly.

Georgia was not certain, but she thought she saw the empress whisk away an errant tear, too.

"Now that I have distributed my largesse—excluding you, Cornelius, for you need nothing but my everlasting thanks—I shall go back to work. I am sure there is a diplomat sitting about somewhere, kicking his heels waiting to speak to me." With a groan, she took Landgräfin Winter's arm and walked out of the saloon and down the gangway, where Georgia distinctly heard one of the ladies say, "Oh, Ma'am, you've been ever so long. There have been no fewer than five messengers."

And then the Landgräfin's voice. "Ma'am, you're not going to ride that appalling velocipede—Your Imperial Majesty, I beg of you—"

Cora and Marcus broke into giggles, and Georgia could not help it, either. She hurried to the viewing port in time to see the Empress of Prussia speeding away on the velocipede down the broad gravel avenue to the palace, a landau full of ladies-in-waiting in white ruffled dresses in hot pursuit.

Kastanienhof, 4:10 p.m.

Herr Brucker walked across the lawn with a letter on a silver tray, to where Georgia sat dreaming in a canvas chair on the lawn. She had not yet wrapped her mind around the empress's gift, now moored over there beside the lake, as it was slightly too large to fit in the home paddock with *Thetis*.

She and Millie, the joint owners of the latest in flight engineering. The *doyennes* of the loveliest of flying homes. Why, they could sail over the curve of the world to the ends of the earth in perfect comfort, given enough coal, kerosene, and water in the boilers.

It rather beggared the imagination.

She took the letter with a smile of thanks and opened it with a sense of relief at something so prosaic. Or that would have been prosaic, had there not been a crest of a deer and a hawk surmounting a banner engraved upon it. The words

DUCAT QUI PACEM CUPIT were engraved rather sternly on the banner.

Dearest Georgia,

Using my friends and acquaintances with my usual ruthless dispatch, you see I have ferreted out where you have been staying. What are you doing in Bavaria when I invited you to Chateau de Valmy? But perhaps your sudden disappearance from Venice has made all invitations slip your mind, not just the one to tea at our villa on the Grand Canal. Now, you see, you must make up for all these lapses in memory by one grand gesture.

If you do not, I shall be highly offended.

No, that is quite untrue. I shall sniffle and feel sorry for myself and wish we lived nearer each other. While your letters over the years have been by turns the cause of tears and the source of joy, they are no substitute for the two of us laughing like ducks over some silly joke and then having to straighten up and behave like ladies in the presence of gentlemen or company.

Your dear aunt-by-marriage will love it here. We shall dream on the terraces to the sound of bees tumbling in the flowers behind us, the lapping of the waves in the lake before us. Tall glasses of lavender lemonade will sweat in the sun while we make our only decision of the day—whether to swim, or go into the village to buy something we do not need.

Do you like the picture I have painted? The lovely thing is that it is all true. My dear Comte joins me in urging you to come and stay as long as you like.

Your own

Anne MacLeod

Comtesse de Valmy

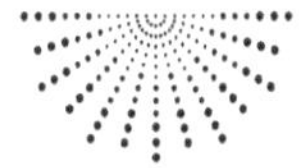

CHAPTER EIGHTEEN

KASTANIENHOF

"May I join you?"

Dustin Seacombe's gravelly voice made Georgia look up from the delights Anne had painted in her letter. Literally painted—a watercolor study of bees enjoying a spike of lavender extended up one side.

"Yes, of course."

"No *of course* about it." He stretched out on the grass beside her chair, his dusty boots crossed at the ankle. "You're not alone much, and when you are, I have to assume you want to stay that way."

"Sometimes." She waggled the letter. "Millie and I have been invited to the Chateau de Valmy, in the south of France. My old schoolmate Anne MacLeod married the count the season after we graduated from St Cecelia's Academy for Young Ladies. He is about twenty years older than she, but from all accounts they have been very happy."

"The south of France." His gaze moved to the floating miracle by the lake, tugging gently on its ropes in the breeze. "Pretty easy to get there now, I guess."

"I have been wondering whether I ought to hire a crew, or teach Millie to pilot as well."

"Both its owners ought to know how to fly it."

She couldn't argue with that. "It's registered with the Naval Office here. I suppose I shall have to re-register it when we go back to England."

He nodded. All civilian airships in England had to be registered so that they could be seconded by the Royal Aeronautic Corps in case of war.

"What about you and Marcus?" she asked, turning the subject. "Your first attempt to go home was interrupted. Does Mr van Meere plan a second?"

"Yep. Tomorrow morning."

The brief words fell like iron cannonbombs through her body—ears, mind, heart, stomach.

"We'll sleep aboard *Foresight* tonight. The winds have swung westerly, so there's no reason to dawdle."

No reason. Only that embrace on the stern platform of *Thetis*.

He rolled to one hip to gaze up at her. The daisy between his fingers fell to the grass. "I don't want to leave you, Georgia. But Cornelius commands my time, and when he says *lift*, me and Marcus, well, we lift."

"I know," she whispered. "Mr Seacombe—"

"Dustin."

The social conversation she had learned over the years failed in the face of his honesty. Finally she found a word or two that made sense. If she dared say them.

She must dare.

"Will you ... add a word or two to Mr van Meere's correspondence with Millie?"

He quirked a craggy eyebrow. "I could add a whole letter. But I understand such a thing means something in your circles." He nodded toward Anne's missive in her lap.

She dared not meet his eyes. "Perhaps. It seems foolish, corresponding with someone on the other side of the world. And yet—"

"And yet." He paused only a moment. "I'll be frank, Georgia—I don't want to leave you. I appreciate that you've been widowed only a year, and I'm not going to rush you into a river you're not willing to swim. But as strange and dangerous as the last several weeks have been, I wouldn't trade them for anything."

Hot color rose into her cheeks. "Letters will seem very tame after these weeks, I agree." Now she did look into his face, just in time to see his cheek dent with that long dimple.

Something danced in his eyes that made her blood tingle. "You haven't read *my* letters."

He rolled to his knees and caught her right hand, turning it to press his lips into her palm. Then, his hand over hers, he cupped it against his cheek. "Cornelius is going to the Symposium of Modern Invention in September. Some English great house is hosting it. Promise me you'll be there."

The palm of her hand had not yet recovered from the caress of his mouth. Neither had the rest of her.

"Yes," she said recklessly. "I'll be there."

"Until then," he said, rising. Then, as if in explanation of such a phrase, he added, "I'm never saying good-bye to you again."

"Until then," she echoed.

And this time when he left her, it felt completely different from all the other times.

I'm never saying good-bye to you again.

It was the most thrilling promise a man had ever made her.

Saturday, May 25, 1895
2:45 p.m.

The empress had seen the LZ-48 stocked with the basics that any ship might carry—tea, flour, sugar, hardtack, fruitcake in airtight tins—and of course the sleeping cabinets had come with fine sheets and thick comforters, towels and cloths and basins. But Louise and Georgia still had the delight of stocking the specifics that suited their taste—eggs, fresh fruit, meat, vegetables, and an array of tiny cakes and tarts courtesy of Cora, who could not imagine anyone traveling without them.

"Must you go?" Louise backed out of a cupboard, where she had been unpacking china bearing the Zeppelin crest into the swinging receptacles that prevented its falling out and breaking during heavy weather. Georgia would replace it with the set of Morvoren china she had brought with her to Langford Park when she was married. Louise looked rested after a night in which she could reasonably expect no attempts at burglary, kidnapping, or murder. "You know you are welcome to stay with us forever, if you want to."

Georgia laughed and kissed her. "We will return, you may be certain of that. Besides, I hear there is a symposium in England in September. Do you plan to attend?"

"Oh, yes. Cornelius and Mr Seacombe are com—" She eyed Georgia, who was valiantly trying not to blush. "But of course you knew that. I take it the correspondence from *Foresight* has doubled?"

Georgia lifted her head and tried for a certain nonchalance. "Possibly."

Louise chuckled. "You are so transparent. But I love you for it. I will leave the two of you now to arrange your nest as you like. Honestly, I don't think Rupert ever set foot in it. The sideboard is empty of whiskey, and even the cooking sherry in the galley is unopened."

Georgia and Millie spent a happy hour moving their traveling closets and valises from the house to the ship, and hanging dresses and blouses in the built-in cabinets with their sinuous carvings of irises and lilies on the doors. The Art Nouveau style suited her perfectly. How clever of the designers at the Zeppelin Airship Works to take beauty into account as well as utility!

At length their empty luggage was stowed in the hold. "Our two traveling closets looked rather small and forlorn in all that space," Georgia remarked as they returned to the main saloon.

"You shall simply have to purchase a two-piston landau to fill it," Millie said flippantly.

"Remind me to take that up with Teddy," she said with a laugh. "Goodness, what will he say when he sees *this* bobbing in the home paddock?"

"Be careful he doesn't fly away in it," Millie warned. "Her, I mean. I must remember to refer to this vessel as *her*."

"She doesn't have a name," Georgia said suddenly. "We cannot very well fly about calling her *LZ-48*, now, can we?"

"It is a mouthful. LZ … hmm. *Elsa?*"

But a tingling shower of certainty had just passed through Georgia's entire body. "No, Millie. There is only one person for whom I wish to name this ship, but you must agree. And wholeheartedly, too."

Millie looked a little alarmed. "Please tell me it is not your late mother."

"Heavens, no. I should be constantly looking around for the woman, not the ship. No. It is a name that comes to my lips all too often. A name I should have been able to speak a dozen times a day for the last eleven years."

Millie's fingers went to her own lips, and her eyes welled with tears.

"She would have loved this ship. Loved traveling with us during school holidays. She and Cora and Marcus would have been the best of friends."

"Oh, Georgia. It is perfect."

Georgia looked up, as though she could see through the false ceiling into the struts and the gasbags, the ropes and the canvas—all the unseen strength that would take them into the next adventure.

"Is it all right with you, dear airship, that we call you after my daughter? Will you answer to *Helena*?"

Perhaps a breeze caught the ship and made it rise just a little. Perhaps the automaton intelligence system was more intelligent than they knew. But *Helena* pulled at her mooring irons like a girl on tiptoe, arms outflung, ready to fly the moment they gave the word.

"We lift tomorrow," Millie whispered. "We must not keep her waiting."

The tears overflowed down Georgia's cheeks as she

wrapped an arm about Millie's waist. The skies to the south were clear, the winds, as Dustin had said, westerly.

"Tomorrow we set our course for France," she agreed when she could speak. "We three. Together always."

THE END

AFTERWORD

A NOTE FROM SHELLEY

Dear reader,

I hope you have enjoyed *The Automaton Empress*, and our continuing adventures in the Magnificent Devices world via the Lady Georgia Brunel Mysteries. Georgia and Millie's adventures will continue in book three, *The Engineer's Nemesis*. Here is a sneak peek:

A chateau in sunny Provence should have meant a holiday, but murder casts long shadows...

Lady Georgia and Millie Brunel are invited to the Chateau de Valmy by Anne MacLeod, the comtesse, an old school friend of Georgia's. In Provence, Anne assures them, they will find sunshine, the scent of lavender, wonderful meals, and a respite from danger.

But before a week has passed, Anne is prostrate with grief. Her husband the comte is dead, and Georgia and Millie find evidence that suggests his death wasn't a natural one. Anne begs them not to involve the local *gendarmes*—the family will be publicly shamed, and their primary suspect, of course, will be Anne herself. With no help forthcoming, then, it is up to Georgia and Millie to discover who could have done this terrible thing. Is someone in the chateau holding a fatal grudge? Or is Anne hiding a secret? Because murder is always about money, power, revenge ... or love.

The Engineer's Nemesis is the third novel in the Lady Georgia Brunel Mysteries series set in the Magnificent Devices steampunk world. Though the books can be read as standalones, there are threads of love and family running through them all. No strong language, just a very proper kiss or two and a satisfying solution.

If this is your first visit to my alt-history world, I hope you will begin your own adventures with the first books in my three connected steampunk series:

- *The Emperor's Aeronaut (The Regent's Devices, 1819)*
- *Lady of Devices (Magnificent Devices, 1889)*
- *The Bride Wore Constant White (Mysterious Devices, 1895)*

I invite you to visit my website, www.shelleyadina.com, to subscribe to my newsletter at https://www.subscribepage.com/shelley-adina, browse my backlist, and learn more about my books. Or visit moonshellbooks.com to buy directly from me. Welcome to the flock!

ALSO BY SHELLEY ADINA

STEAMPUNK

The Magnificent Devices series

Lady of Devices

Her Own Devices

Magnificent Devices

Brilliant Devices

A Lady of Resources

A Lady of Spirit

A Lady of Integrity

A Gentleman of Means

Devices Brightly Shining (Christmas novella)

Fields of Air

Fields of Iron

Fields of Gold

Carrick House (novella)

Selwyn Place (novella)

Holly Cottage (novella)

Gwynn Place (novella)

Acorn (novella)

Aster (novella)

Iris (novella)

Rosa (novella)

The Mysterious Devices series

The Bride Wore Constant White

The Dancer Wore Opera Rose

The Matchmaker Wore Mars Yellow

The Engineer Wore Venetian Red

The Judge Wore Lamp Black

The Professor Wore Prussian Blue

The Lady Georgia Brunel Mysteries

"The Air Affair" (prequel short story)

The Clockwork City

The Automaton Empress

The Engineer's Nemesis

The Aeronaut's Heir

The Texican Tinkerer

The Wounded Airship

The Regent's Devices series with R.E. Scott

The Emperor's Aeronaut

The Prince's Pilot

The Lady's Triumph

The Pilot's Promise (novella)

The Aeronaut's Heart (novella in anthology)

ABOUT THE AUTHOR

Shelley Adina is the author of nearly 60 novels published by Harlequin, Warner, Hachette, and Moonshell Books, Inc., her own independent press. She writes steampunk adventure and mystery as Shelley Adina, and as Adina Senft, is the *USA Today* bestselling author of Amish women's fiction.

She holds a PhD in Creative Writing from Lancaster University in the UK. She won RWA's RITA Award® in 2005, and was a finalist in 2006. She appeared in the 2016 documentary film *Love Between the Covers*, is a popular speaker and convention panelist, and has been a guest on many podcasts, including Worldshapers and Realm of Books.

When she's not writing, Shelley is usually quilting, sewing historical costumes, or enjoying the garden with her flock of rescued chickens.

Shelley loves to talk with readers about books, chickens, and costuming!

shelleyadina.com
moonshellbooks.com